ONE NIGHT.
ONE MISTAKE.
TWO VERY ATTRACTIVE
COWBOYS.

Fires Creek

D.M. HENDERSON

ISBN: 978-1-7641927-1-2

Cover by RJ Creatives

Art by @_art_valerey_ & @teoctobart

Edited by Erin Page of Erin Writes Romance

Formatted by D.M. Henderson

This is for everyone who wanted *both* cowboys.

'Love isn't something you find. Love is something that finds
you.' – *Loretta Young*

PLAYLIST:

River's Song – Love in a Country Town – Lane Pittman

Jonas's Song – Hard to Love – Lee Brice

Teddy's Song – Sounds Like Something I'd Do – Drake Milligan

Lonely Road – MGK & Jelly Roll

Going Nowhere Fast – Lane Pittman

I Had Some Help – Post Malone & Morgan Wallen

The Kind of Love We Make – Luke Combs

Nice to meet you – Myles Smith & Lainey Wilson

Let's Get Lost – Lane Pittman

You look like you love me – Ella Langley & Riley Green

Bottoms Up – Brantley Gilbert

Austin (Boots stop workin') – Dasha

You Found Yours – Luke Combs

Forever After All – Luke Combs

SENSITIVE CONTENT
Please Read

I have taken great care to ensure any potential content warnings have been mentioned. If anything has been missed, please don't hesitate to reach out.

While *Fires Creek* is not a dark novella, it does touch on topics that may not be for everyone. If you at any point don't feel comfortable with the content within these pages, please don't continue. Your mental health is important. That being said, I hope you love River, Teddy, and Jonas's story as much as I do.

Fires Creek contains the following subject matters:

Non-abusive alcohol use, death of a parent (off page historical), drug use, graphic, detailed, on page sexual acts, (including but not limited to: MF, MMF, anal play, verbal and physical degradation, double penetration and pegging) Bull riding accident, minor medical procedures (depicted on page).

AUTHORS NOTE
Australian-Isms

Fires Creek is written in Australian English. You may notice some minor spelling differences from US/UK English.

Some of these that you may notice are: jewellery vs jewelry, dialled vs dialed and centre vs center. As *Fires Creek* is set in Australia, you'll also find interesting slang and cultural references.

Some of the fun Aussie words you'll find sprinkled within these pages:

Bloke — An unnamed male, generally a term of endearment

Ute — A utility vehicle. Commonly referred to elsewhere as a 'pickup truck.'

D.M. HENDERSON

Prologue
River

6 months earlier

"Fuck off, Jesse, I don't want to hear it!" I slammed my fist against the counter, and popped the cork out of my second bottle of wine.

"Rivvy, babe, you're not thinking straight. Calm down, we can talk about this," he stammered pathetically. God, he was such a creep. This mother fucker actually thought I was oblivious to the fact he was having an affair at the same time I was watching my mother die. *Prick.*

"Get your shit, and get out!" I shouted, shoving his bag in his face and storming out of the kitchen, locking the bedroom door behind me – bottle of wine, still in hand.

I heard the front door slam a few minutes later, and his stupid hybrid car sped out of the driveway. God, I can't believe I was actually going to marry him. I took another swig from the bottle of cabernet. It would really be better in a glass, but I was beyond caring.

Flopping onto the couch in the corner of my room, I flicked the TV on, only to be met with the Colgate smile of some realtor that called himself 'Link Tyler, Realtor for the Stars.' *Wow, thank you, Link. I will be sure to sell you my soul. Realtor for the Stars, my ass.*

The ad continued and snippets of property previews filled the screen. I was about to click the remote and go to bed, when the most beautiful, old farmhouse that I had ever seen flashed across the screen. Rustic fences scaled their way across fields of well-maintained paddocks. At the end of a long, winding, gravel road sat the huge log-built homestead. A large chimney adorned the rooftop, and a thick cloud of smoke billowed out across the ranges.

Trees in various shapes and sizes, ranging from deep green to burnt orange, lined the property. It looked so *cosy*. The camera scaled across the acreage, showcasing the huge river nearby, the surrounding properties, and the mountain ranges that laid nestled behind the farm. Cattle lowed in nearby paddocks, and the camera panned to a scene of horses galloping across the plains.

"Not to be missed, the infamous Ashwood Manor. If you're looking for adventure, head on down to Fires Creek and check out this pristine property!" came the overly optimistic tone from our buddy, Link, as the ad blared over the TV speakers.

Without taking a second to process what I was doing – or consider that 9:45 pm is probably not an appropriate time for business calls – I dialled Link's number, and in my drunken state, made him an offer he couldn't refuse.

My eyes felt heavy as I woke up, still on the couch, and rubbed the grit of sleep from them. A wet, stained piece of paper with poorly scribbled gibberish was plastered to my coffee table.

Fires Creek?
What the fuck is Fires Creek?
Who the fuck are Link and Carter?
What have I done?

ONE
River

Present Day

As my car chugged through the town square of Fires Creek, I soaked in the abundance of greenery. People wandered through the village hand-in-hand, kids rode their bikes on the sidewalk, there were also a lot of cows.

How the hell did I end up here?

I wasn't a country person.

Have I lost my mind?

The city I lived in was so much bigger, louder, and bustling with opportunities. I found a job almost instantly. The years of online graphic design school, and the 4-hour commute for practical days finally paid off, I guess. I clawed my way up the corporate ladder until I was living comfortably enough to freelance instead. That's where the money was.

Huge corporations paid me through the roof to do menial shit, like logo design and website creation. Being my own boss gave me the freedom to choose my clients and take on pro-bono jobs. I've done quite a lot of work for not-for-profits and charity organisations that couldn't always afford high-end design services, and I had no problem sucking big corporations dry to help the underdog.

The next few years were a blur of pub crawls, one-night stands, and whatever powder the guy I took home was buying that night. Sometimes, there was more than one. Guy that is, not powder. Although...

One night, I met a bloke in a bar – classy, I know – and ended up moving in with him after a few weeks. Jesse proposed within a month of my arrival, and we were all but ready to walk down the aisle. Then, after Mum died, I started drinking, broke off my engagement to that cheating sack of shit, and promptly purchased a fucking *farm*. I don't know why I'd assumed I was the kind of person who could live on a *farm*, let alone *run* a *farm*, but here we are.

I could hear Mum now: "River Carlisle, what's gotten into you? Why do you always have to be so reckless?"

Then, she would kiss my nose and laugh as she recounted some old memory of her and Dad. She'd give me shit about it, but she'd ultimately end up going along with my crazy scheme anyway. I missed her. Mum was always my biggest supporter and cheerleader; although, I know she wished I had settled down a bit more. I was barely 32, I had time. I just wish she did too...

The morning after my delightful phone call with Link, he'd called me to follow-up on my offer. Something about my slurred words and the inappropriate hour of my phone call apparently made him consider that I may not have been entirely sober. According to him I had talked his ear off, placed a ludicrous offer on the property, and promptly fallen asleep on the phone. Definitely *not* my finest moment. Most people get a piercing or change their hair after a breakup. But not me, nope. I get blind-drunk and buy a *farm*.

I had always been on the frugal side, invested and saved, so the outlay for the farm really didn't set me back too much financially, thank God. I suppose one of the perks of my job is that I made damn good money. That didn't mean I spent it wisely... Like the time I bought 9 different leather jackets because I couldn't decide. Or the espresso machine I got online that I *still* don't know how to use. Don't even get me started on the amount of bar tabs I had covered...

I'd set up a coffee date with Link and we sat down to discuss the logistics of the settlement. He was actually surprisingly down-to-earth. I was expecting a flamboyant douche-canoe, but I was met with a humble country boy.

He explained the history of the farm, detailing how it belonged to the oldest family in Fires Creek, and how their son, Jonas, had taken over his father's role as foreman after he passed.

All Link said was that the current owner of the property had no interest in their investment anymore and had always been a silent developer from interstate. He didn't elaborate on what happened to the owner or Jonas's Dad, but I had a feeling it was a pivotal moment for the town, and maybe not the best kind.

I had sat on the corner of my purple quilt, staring blankly at the property ownership document in my hand. I actually did it. I bought a fucking *farm*. My hands trembled as my eyes trailed over the paperwork, my mind taking its time to catch-up on the series of events that had unravelled over the past few days. I didn't know what to expect, as I started packing up my entire life into a suitcase and prepared to leave the city behind.

I had put aside enough money to set me up for at least 6 months while I figured out staffing, settled in, and wrapped my head around what the hell I was supposed to be doing in Fires Creek. First thing Monday, I was making an appointment with whoever I needed to and discussing my options. For now, I wanted to settle in and introduce myself to the foreman and his assistant. My new *employees?*

I had just made the right-hand turn onto the winding road leading up the mountain, towards *the farm*, when panic struck. What the actual *fuck* was I doing here? I had never even heard of Fires Creek until 6 months ago. So, I did the only rational thing I could think of: I gulped my panic down, and parked my Mini-Cooper at the front entrance to Ashwood Manor, letting myself soak in in the beauty of the rolling hills and fresh-cut grass.

As I grabbed the now lukewarm coffees that rested in the cupholders of my car, I couldn't help but laugh at this entire situation. All I knew is that I was meeting some bloke called Jonas – he was the foreman, and a bit of a grouch, apparently. Well, that's what the real estate guy, our buddy, Link, told me.

I took a deep breath and let my feet lead the way as I made the unfamiliar walk down to the rusted shed out the back. My eyes trailed over the looming, black clouds on the horizon. The crisp, mountain air was delicious and clear, despite the storm rolling in from the south; I just hoped the storm held off until nightfall, it was already getting late...

Who gets drunk and buys a house? I was completely convinced that I was making an insane decision, but fuck it, I was already here. I took a final, deep breath and lifted my chin, feigning confidence as I strode towards my new life.

Well, here goes nothin'.

"Howdy, boys. Looks like you could use some company."

Two

Jonas

"For fuck's sake, Teddy, could you *please* stop with that god awful music? I can't hear myself think," I bellowed from beneath the hood of my ute.

Ever since I could remember, Theodore had been a right pain in my ass – which didn't get any better when the little shit moved in. I still remember the day Mum brought him home from the hospital after the fall. She had been gone 3 years now. Dad followed not long after; he was never the same after she passed.

"Calm down, ya grumpy old prick," came his reply.

I put down my spanner and turned my gaze to my *brother*. I suppose he was in a way. Mum took him in when he was 16, after the accident, and he's just sort of been around since. Teddy drove me nuts – but this place sure would be quiet without him. Back then, he was so young, but so damn reckless. Fearless is probably a better word for it – he just loved to ride. Now, at almost 30, since he was medically retired; he stole my smokes, drank my whiskey, and couldn't keep his hands to himself. The never-ending line of men and women parading through the house at all hours of the night gave that away.

I opened my mouth to shoot Teddy a snappy remark – I was barely 3 years older than him; he could fuck off with this old man shit – but a sudden thud from behind the shed pulled me up short. "What the hell was that?" Teddy shouted, closing the gap between us in three long strides and pausing for a moment.

My German Shepherd, Alex, came bounding out from the bushes with a damn rabbit in his mouth. "Bloody hell, Al, knock it off. You scared the crap outta me." I laughed, tousling the hair around his neck and peeling the animal from his jaw.

The rabbit scampered away, leaving Alex whimpering in defeat as he turned towards his favourite spot in the shed and curled up on his make-shift dog bed: one of Dad's old shirts. Alex was a gentle old bugger. He never hurt the animals, just carried them in like they were gonna unpack and move in or something. I reckon he just missed my old man. I missed the old man too...

The subtle smell of coffee wafted through the air, filling my nose as the faint sound of footsteps grew closer. "Howdy boys, looks like you could use some company," came a soft, polished accent. Then, *she* emerged, coffee in tow, and a smile so bright it put the town square Christmas lights to shame.

Her hair fell in thick, loose waves around her shoulders, and it was the colour of those bricks you see in well-built houses. Fuck, I suck at this. She was a redhead, and she was *incredible*. Her smile crept from the corners of her mouth and her dimples plunged into her cheeks. God, she was gorgeous.

"Coffee, boys?" she asked, as if we knew who the fuck she was and why she'd just turned up at the house.

"Hell yeah!" Teddy replied, not bothering to ask her any further questions. *Idiot.*

I studied her as she handed the coffee to my brother, tugging on my shirt – which at this point was more black than green, thanks to this stupid ute and its never-ending oil leak – and took a few steps forward, closing the gap between us. I puffed out my chest a little. I was not exactly Jason Momoa, but this woman was tiny, and I was anything but. The years of farm work had definitely paid off. I had never been in such good shape. Still, I could stand to lay off the booze...

Teddy interrupted my train of thought as an inhumane splutter exploded from his lips, and coffee covered the ground in front of him.

"It's fuckin' cold," he exclaimed, his brow furrowed with disapproval.

The pretty redhead smirked, rolling her eyes as she purred, "Oh, is it? What a damn shame."

"Uh, I might pass on the cuppa. Thanks... And who are you exactly?" I asked.

"Well, sugar, if I tell you that, it'll ruin the fun, won't it? You must be Jonas." Her voice was as sweet as sin, dripping from her plump pink lips. Alex leapt from his bed and ran to her, allowing her to lavish him with pats. He flopped down and rolled over, showing her his belly with his tongue hanging from his mouth. *Useless little sook.*

I don't know if it was her outfit, or the fact she just *looked* like a city girl, but I knew in my gut she must be the chick who bought the farm. I wasn't expecting her until Monday, and she was *not* what I was expecting when Link said someone from out of town had bought the place. I wasn't expecting someone young, let alone someone who fucking looked like *her*. From her perky tits, to the award-winning smile she flashed me, I knew I was absolutely fucked.

Her wild, auburn hair was vivid and captivating against her porcelain skin. The waves of red rested messily against the black fabric that covered her neck and shoulders, leaving only her cleavage exposed. Gold chains in various styles hung from her neck and fell just before her breasts. A deep, green corset accentuated every damn curve on this woman's body.

Dark, intricate ink cascaded across the delicate flesh of her forearm and two bands of barbed wire wrapped around her other arm. Her skirt clung to her milky thighs for dear life. Her toenails were painted the perfect shade of navy to compliment the gold jewellery that adorned every bloody surface imaginable. She must be some sort of magpie. A very, sexy, magpie. *God, what the fuck is wrong with me?* Before I could open my mouth to speak, Teddy interrupted my thoughts with his bloody big mouth and ruined it.

THREE
Teddy

14 years ago. Age 16

My head hit the dirt with an almighty thud as my wrist gave out and I tumbled down from the back of Terror. He was a good bull, young and fit; but so was I. I was in my fucking *prime*. Apparently, that didn't mean shit tonight. He was out for blood, and I was the unlucky bastard who drew his card. *Next time, boy.*

I felt the air leave my lungs as my body slammed into the cold, hard floor of the arena. My third championship was slipping away, and there wasn't a damn thing I could do about it. I would be out for the season, maybe more, after a fall like this. *My first fall.*

"Someone call a fucking ambulance, he's down!" A panicked scream came from somewhere in the arena.

Voices echoed all around me, a sharp ringing radiated through my ears. My eyes were gritty and heavy as my vision blurred, and my surroundings became nothing but dimly lit shadows.

"Teddy! TEDDY! Talk to me!"

Link?

"Is he okay?" Another familiar voice cut through my fucking ears.

Hannah?

"Fuck knows, he's breathing though!"

"Get the nurse! Where's Maggie?" A panicked reply came from someone in the crowd.

Maggie?

Who the hell is Maggie?

Why wasn't anyone coming for me?

Feeling myself weaving in and out of consciousness, I let my eyes close as tears welled in my ducts and threatened to escape down my cheeks. *No, you fucking don't.* The ringing sound grew louder and louder; it was starting to hurt. Everything was starting to hurt. I had no idea who was gathered around me, but I could make out voices arguing over what had just happened.

I tried to open my eyes, but they refused. So, I just lay there, waiting to die. I mean, I don't exactly know if I was going to die, but I sure as hell wanted to. My ribs were on fire, my heart felt like it was going to burst out of my chest, and the fucking incessant ringing noise was giving me a violent headache. I felt a sudden, sharp prick inside the crook of my left elbow as a soft hand found my cheek.

"It's okay, Theodore, you're safe," a gentle, feminine voice echoed through the ringing. Her hands stroked my face slowly, and everything faded to black.

"Good morning, Mr James," that same, gentle voice chimed through my ears.

My tired eyes slowly fluttered open, allowing me to take in my surroundings. *I was in the fucking hospital.* I was hooked up to several obnoxiously loud machines and had cannulas inserted into my wrist and elbow. *Great.*

The nurse gracefully entered my room, carrying a tray of medicine and a bottle of water. She had little pink ponies on her scrubs, and her grey hair was pulled neatly off her face.

"What happened?" I asked, wondering how I ended up here.

"Here, son. Take these, they'll help with the pain." She handed me the pills, which I downed instantly with the water. Everything. Fucking. Hurt.

"Thank you, ma'am."

"Oh, please, it's Maggie. Maggie Carter," she said, smiling at me and taking my empty glass. "You had quite the tumble, dear. Had the whole town worried." She said, her voice soft and kind.

"Yeah, feels that way. What happened to Terror?"

"He's back at the Jensen's, ready to buck another day. Unfortunately, my dear, I don't think we can say the same for you. Your surgery went well, but the damage to your wrist is undeniable. You also fractured multiple ribs, tore some ligaments in your shoulder, and had quite a nasty concussion," she explained.

Maggie checked my cannulas and topped up the bags of whatever shit was in the IV's as she answered my question. Her eyes narrowed as she checked my blood pressure. She shook her head and retested before taking her notes. I watched her eyes scan over my injuries, her hands scribbling more notes onto my chart.

"So, what does that mean?" I asked, my mind racing in a panic.

She stopped prodding around and sat on the shitty hospital chair next to my bed. Taking my hand in hers, she murmured. "You may need to rethink your career prospects, my dear." Her soothing voice did nothing to lessen the blow of her words.

I lay there, swollen, sore, and absolutely fucking furious as I absorbed the information Maggie just divulged. It felt like a fuck tonne of cement had been dumped on my chest to slowly suffocate me. I felt my lungs heave as I desperately tried to inhale oxygen.

"Woah now, easy honey," she murmured, her soft hands meeting my face. She gently stroked my cheek and guided me back to reality.

"They said you had no next of kin to call when you were admitted," she commented, although it was really more of a question.

"Nope. I'm emancipated," I offered in reply, trying to steady my breath.

"I'm sorry to hear that."

"Yeah, me too."

I told her about my parents. How they dumped me at school one day when I was 12 and never came back. I was in and out of foster homes from then until my 15th birthday. At that point, the school's social worker helped me find a lawyer, and file for emancipation.

My parents didn't even bother attending the hearing, although the judge told me they'd received the summons. Fuck knows where they went or why they left me, but I didn't need them. I didn't need anyone. Until now.

I started bull-riding at 14, joined the rodeo circuit and hit the ground running. After my second title belt, I had made enough money to buy a house and get my shit together. But despite being emancipated, I was 15 at the time, so I couldn't do shit. I had rented a house off one of the blokes from the circuit, bought a beat-up Ford the moment I could and never looked back. Sure, I couldn't *legally* drive, but like that ever stopped me.

Maggie rose from her seat on my bed and placed her hand gently on top of mine. The simple gesture gave me a sense of hope, of comfort. She told me she'd be back in an hour to check on me, encouraging me to get some rest. I wondered what it must be like to have a mother. What would it feel like to be loved?

"Mrs Carter?"

"Yes, Theodore?"

"Thank you. For being so kind."

"You're welcome, dear." She turned on her heels and left me alone with my thoughts.

The sharp beeping of my heart-rate monitor snapped me out of my sleep, and I pried my eyes open. I squinted as the harsh, fluorescent lights assaulted my weary eyes. I looked down to inspect myself. This was the first time since that night I had really taken a moment to assess my surroundings and process what had happened. I had been here for a fucking week and was still in a state of shock. *Get over it, Teddy.*

Flashbacks of the fall invaded my head as my eyes trailed over my bruised legs and the lacerations coating my skin. I had a gauze wrapped over my left calf; I assumed that was from the fence that almost impaled me as I tumbled from the bull. I took in the plaster cast that adorned my right wrist. I tried, and failed, to grip the frame of my hospital bed and sit up. Pain shot through my arm, and it felt like a thousand stinging needles embedding into me. *Fuck this.* I pressed the call button and Maggie appeared within a few minutes, more pills and water in tow.

"Morning, sunshine," she cooed, taking a seat on the bed beside me and handing me the tray.

"Don't you ever get a day off, Mrs Carter?" I gave her a bashful smile and cocked my eyebrow at her playfully, then downed the pills with a large gulp of water.

"I go home from time to time," she laughed. "In fact, my son, Jonas, is only a few years older than you. I have asked him to come in today to keep you company."

"You didn't have to do that, Mrs Carter," I replied, taking another sip of water, feeling like she just ordered me a babysitter. At least the cool rush of liquid instantly eased the pain in my ribs.

"He's a lovely boy; he helps us around the farm. I thought you may have some things in common. He rides too, horses mostly. He said he knew of you from the rodeo circuit," she announced proudly.

The door to my hospital room creaked open, and a tall, stocky teenager appeared in the door frame. He stood there, looking rough with a sheepish expression plastered on his face, before he shuffled into the room.

"Uh, hey. I'm Jonas," came his deep, gravelly voice. Deeper than you'd expect from a teenager.

I don't know what the fuck was happening, but that voice and his smile sent shivers down my spine and straight to my dick. *This man was fucking gorgeous.*

Jonas stayed with me for most of the day, telling me stories about his time on the farm. His eyes danced when he spoke of the horses, and his lips quivered when he laughed. Although he was only a few years older than me, he looked like a man despite only being 19. His tanned skin was slightly withered, his body toned and muscular from the hours spent working in the sun. Subtle smile lines creeped across his face, almost hidden beneath his beard.

I found myself thinking about him long after he'd left, wondering if he'd come back and visit me again. Although, I hadn't really asked him to. Maybe I was overthinking things. *Shit.*

Maggie quietly creeped back into my room holding a thick manilla folder. She took her usual spot next to me on the bed, and with a cheeky smile, she asked, "Theodore James, how would you like to become a Carter?"

FOUR
Jonas

14 years ago. Age 19

We'd been home for an hour, and I was still completely shocked that Mum brought Teddy home to live with us. He seemed cool, but I wasn't used to having another person here. Aside from the farm hands that came in to help during peak season, it was just me, Mum, and Dad. We'd lived in Ashwood Manor my whole life. Dad was the foreman, and someday, I would follow in his footsteps.

I had grown up on the back of a horse, learning to ride as soon as I could walk. Riding was second nature to me. Dad spent my childhood teaching me everything I needed to know and then some. By the age of 12, I was able to fix any machinery just as well as I could tie my damn shoelaces. Not that Ariats had shoelaces...

I knew of Teddy from the rodeo circuit. Where he rode bulls, I rode horses. He was new to the scene, clocking his second win last year at only 15. I was a few years older so we mixed in different crowds, but his reputation was undeniable. A young, upcoming rider with a fearless outlook and an unstoppable spirit. It really was a damn shame his career ended the way it did. He was a bloody good rider. But all it took was one bad fall and you were totally fucked.

"Do you need some help unpacking?" I asked.

"Ummm, nah. I should be a'right. My wrist feels pretty good today, thanks."

"Uh, yeah, okay. See you later then," I said, chewing the inside of my cheek.

I walked back down through the hallway, scuffing my boots along the floorboards. I couldn't stop thinking about him. The way his thick eyebrows cocked when he smiled. How his Wranglers fit perfectly on his hips. His shaggy, blond hair. That fucking smile.

I shook my head, descending the staircase as the intrusive thoughts invaded my head. I found myself thinking about him more than I cared to admit, and I couldn't help but wonder if he was thinking about me too.

FIVE
Teddy

Present Day

Jonas always had a stick up his ass; dude needed to get laid. He was interrogating this chick like he was a cop. I don't understand him sometimes. She was hot as hell and came bearing coffee. Who cares what her name is? She's got good tits, a pretty smile, and I bet her tattooed fingers would look beautiful wrapped around my cock as I throat fucked her. I shuddered at the thought, my dick twitching against my jeans.

"The name is Theodore James, milady. But I'll let you call me Teddy, or you can call me tonight," I said, faking a dramatic bow and gesturing towards my brother. "This piece of shit is Jonas, he doesn't bite... much." I gave her a wink, just for some extra flair. "And that dopey bastard," I said pointing to Alex, who was curled up on his bed. "Is the Almighty Alex! What brings you to Fires Creek? You don't look local."

She didn't reply, just stared at us with those delicious honey-coloured eyes. None of us tried to fill the silence, so I studied her form. Her hair sat just above her waist, which was perfectly squeezed into a black leather skirt that fell mid-way down her thighs. Her flesh was soft and milky, a stark contrast from her flaming hair and the pots of gold that lurked beneath her lashes. I trailed my eyes down her frame, from her tiny button nose to the Doc Marten sandals that displayed her perfectly manicured toes, adorned with several gold rings. A delicate, gold anklet just peeking out from the thick, leather ankle strap.

My eyes wandered up her thighs. A deep green corset cinched tightly at her waist was paired with a black turtleneck with a large cut-out across her chest. The apples of her breasts bulged above the ruffles on the corset. How a piece of clothing could cover so much skin but be so damn sexy is beyond me. Gold chains adorned both her neck and the corset that clung to her curves so perfectly. Intricate tendrils of ink snaked their way up her forearms until they met the array of gold rings scattered across her slender fingers.

What was I saying before about those fingers?

I was so fucked...

Jonas chose that exact moment to interrupt my viewing experience. "Ah, you must be the new landlord."

Ah, shit.

SIX
River

T eddy Carter was *fucking delicious*. He'd been eye-fucking me since I got here. I won't lie, the attention didn't bother me in the slightest. There was something about him that drew me in. Like I was being involuntarily pulled to him or something.

We let the silence linger for a moment, before Jonas pointed towards the house, gesturing for me to follow. He led the way and held the door open for me; Teddy followed close behind. I could practically feel his eyes lingering on my ass as we made our way into the kitchen.

Huge mosaic tiles lined the splashback, meeting the deep wood-grained benches that occupied the space. There were empty bottles of bourbon and whiskey stacked in one corner, alongside several packets of cigarettes. The kitchen adjoined a large, cosy-looking sitting room that felt like it was pasted straight out of a Country Living catalogue. I was actually surprised at how beautiful the Manor was considering it was run by two gruff cowboys.

Jonas sighed, pulling a bottle of Maker's Mark from the bar. He pulled out three crystal glasses, stopping to gaze in my direction, before pouring the malt liquor into the glasses before him and sliding them down the bench towards Teddy and me. He filled his own glass, raising it to us in a single nod, before downing the contents in one gulp.

Jonas topped up his glass, and Teddy flashed me a wicked grin before quipping to him, "Well, since she's the boss around here now, maybe we should teach her how to *work*." His voice was gravely and thick with lust as he wiggled his eyebrows.

"Knock it off Teddy, she wanted a job and a home, not a fucking venereal disease," Jonas growled, pouring us another round.

"I will have you know, dearest Joney, that I am a fucking saint," came Teddy's reply. He flopped himself onto the worn, leather armchair in the corner of the room and pulled a pack of cigarettes from his top pocket, along with a gold engraved lighter. He sparked his cigarette and took a long, deep drag. His expression calmed as he inhaled the tendrils of smoke.

"Yeah, and I am Hugh fuckin' Jackman," Jonas replied, a deep, warm laugh seeping from his mouth. He shook his head, looking down at his empty glass, and mumbled something incoherent. Then, he turned on the heels of his well-worn boots and made his way to the matching leather armchair in the sitting room, sighing again as he settled into it. "So, what brings you to Fires Creek? And why'd you buy the farm?"

"It's kind of a long story. My mum died, and I just got out of a really intense relationship. Apparently, I make interesting life choices after a bottle of wine," I replied, sheepishly.

"Well, River," Teddy purred. "I, for one, am so *glad* we have a fresh face in this place. I get sick of looking at Jonas's ugly mug every day." He took a long sip of whiskey and another drag of his cigarette. As he ran his fingers through his hair, a devilish grin crept over his mouth, and his eyes never left mine.

We sat there for a while, drinking and talking. The boys told me what I was in for, assuring me they'd 'show me the ropes'. Jonas recounted a typical day, explaining how the feed cycles worked, which stock belonged in which paddock. He even went as far as to give me a rundown of the neighbours and made sure I knew the ins and outs of small-town politics. According to the boys, our neighbour, Brenda Hartford, was around once a week to check on the cattle she was agisting here and usually came bearing casseroles.

I could listen to Jonas read me a phonebook, honestly. His voice was so soothing, so *familiar*. It didn't hurt that he was fucking delicious either. *What was in the water in this place? Did hot, charming cowboys grow on trees here? Get it together, woman.*

"So do you guys come up to the main house often?" I asked, taking another sip of my drink.

"Come up here? Peach, we *live* here." Teddy stated.

"You fucking what?"

"The Manor, we live in it. I have since I was born," Jonas offered, an oddly sombre expression washed over his face.

"The previous owner was never here, so when my dad, Frank, was hired as Foreman, our family were given the house. When my parents adopted Teddy, he moved in too. My family has been here for over 50 years," Jonas continued.

"So... we're technically *housemates?*" I asked. At this point, what the fuck else was I supposed to do? Kick them out? *Sure, that'd go down well.*

Teddy's eyes lingered on me as he quietly sipped his whiskey. The way his full lips curled over the ornamental glass sent pools of heat to my core. This man was somehow both adorable and devastatingly sexy.

"Is that a problem for you, River Carlisle?" Teddy questioned, each word enunciated slowly. It felt more like a challenge than a question. The way my name fell from his lips was dizzying. *Alright, Theodore. Game on, let's play.*

"Only if you promise to be a good boy, Theodore." I let the words drip slowly from my mouth, careful to leave him right on the edge, exactly where I wanted him.

He smirked in approval, leaning back in his chair and resting his boots against the firm, oak table before him. The dark brown leather of his boots was coated in dust and worn at every angle. Scuff marks covered the heel entirely, and the stitching was coming away towards the toe. They were beautiful, like their wearer. A large, flashy belt buckle with a gold longhorn peeked from beneath the fabric of his shirt, which was lazily tucked into one side of his jeans.

As the night went on and alcohol consumed me, the more I wished they'd show me their ropes - or tie me up in them. *Knock it off. I cannot be having these thoughts. I am their boss, for God's sake.*

"You need to learn how to ride a damn horse!" Teddy slurred, leaning forward and winking at me.

"I can ride a horse, thank you very much. It's just... been a while."

"Well, you might be able to ride a horse, sweet cheeks, but can ya' ride a cowboy? YEEHAAAW!" He yelled, standing to his feet and thrusting his hips wildly. *Idiot.*

"Fuck me dead, Teddy, give her a break." Jonas sighed, throwing a pillow towards him and shaking his head. "Sorry, River," he offered.

"I'm a big girl, Jonas. I think I can handle a cowboy, or two. Although, I've never had my very own before." I giggled, my teeth sinking into my lower lip ever so slightly as my eyes met his.

Jonas's cheeks flushed crimson, his hand raised as if he was going to speak, but the words never came. *Nothing to say, hey? You aren't like your brother then.*

"Alright boys, I'm just gonna go get my stuff and unpack. It's almost dark out, and this storm seems to be setting in." I confidently pressed my hands against my skirt as I stood up, downed my drink, and gathered myself to leave.

I made my way through the cosy, rustic halls of the Manor, soaking in the intricate art that lined the walls. There's stunning landscape paintings of galloping horses and rolling hills, and I spotted an old photo of Teddy standing in some sort of pen, next to a gigantic bull. He had a satisfied smile plastered across his boyish face. A thick, bronze plate adorned the frame reading: *'Theodore James. 14y/o Novice. 1ˢᵗ Place Professional Bull Riding, Wattle Ridge.'* I couldn't help but smile. Even as a teenager, he still had that same cheeky look about him.

The storm was rolling in fast, and the crisp air bit at my face as I stepped outside. The flood lights shone over the manor, casting thick, ominous shadows across the yard. I hadn't realised that Teddy followed me out to the car until he cleared his throat behind me. I turned to see a crooked smile creeping across his mouth. He propped an arm against the roof of my Mini Cooper and leant into me, his smoky eyes dancing as they met mine.

"You need some help there, Peach?"

"What's with the Peach shit?" I asked. An overwhelming, gravitational pull stopped me from looking anywhere but his eyes. His smoky, green eyes. *I was fucked.*

He moved in closer, the whiskey lingering on his breath, intoxicating me as he invaded my space and murmured slowly. "I like it. It suits you. Peach, like your pretty, pink, cunt."

He didn't wait for me to reply. He just winked at me and opened the door, revealing my things packed neatly in the backseat. This man was absolutely gorgeous, and, apparently, that meant I had forgotten how to breathe. Or, you know, be normal.

"What's the matter, River? Ain't never let a cowboy get under your skin?" he asked, smirking as his eyes darkened.

"And what makes you think that *you* are going to get under my skin, *Theodore?*" I replied, pressing myself against him ever so slightly. His eyes twinkled and tiny flecks of brown danced around his pupils, enhancing the iridescent shade of green that lay beneath them as they bore into me with the question, and I cocked my brow up in a challenge.

That was clearly all the invitation he needed. His hands slid through my hair, as he plunged his tongue into my mouth. He tasted like whiskey and cigarettes. "God, you taste so fuckin' good, darlin'," he moaned into me.

I don't know if it's all the shit that happened the last few years – or if I just needed to get laid – but I had no intention of stopping this man. The clouds grew darker behind us as our mouths crashed together fiercely, hungrily. He wrapped his hands around my thighs, sliding them up my ass as he lifted me around his waist, never breaking our kiss. My skirt rode up my thighs, and his erection pressed against my core. He swirled his hips and ground into me, the car providing the perfect balance for friction.

"Mmm, sweet girl," his gravelly voice beckoned me as he stroked the hair from my cheek. He pressed his rough lips to my throat and sucked on my tender flesh, hard enough to mark me with his touch. I was absolutely feral for this man.

"God, Teddy, yes!" I panted against his shoulders.

He quickened the pace of his grinding hips, and I slipped my hands between us. Fumbling with his ostentatious belt buckle, I flicked the clasp open and yanked at the button of his jeans. Pulling his belt out of the loops and discarding it on the dirt driveway, I pressed my mouth back to his.

He winced as the belt hit the dirt with a thud before pulling his lips from mine and groaning, "Ugh, be gentle with her."

"Her?" I asked.

"Traditionally, one doesn't throw a man's belt in the dirt, Peach."

"Shit. Sorry."

He growled and his mouth again met mine in a kiss that was hungry and demanding. There was nothing soft or gentle about how this man was claiming me.

"Wait, are we really doing this?" I asked. Pausing for a moment to assess the situation I had somehow found myself in – mere hours after arriving at this place I was face battling a fucking cowboy in the driveway.

As if reading my mind, Teddy asked, "If 'by doing this' you mean are you dry humping a near stranger against your car, in a driveway, in a storm, then, yeah, I guess we are." He almost kissed me again, but paused. "Wait, do you want me to stop? You seemed like yo—"

"Fuck no" I replied without letting him finish, returning my mouth to his as he pressed his length against my throbbing pussy. With my thighs wrapped tightly around his hips, Teddy started to carry me back towards the house.

"I need to taste you, Peach," he moaned into me, kissing me deeper.

Teddy walked me straight to his room and threw me on his bed, ripping my skirt from my body before nestling between my thighs and plunging his tongue into my centre. He moaned against my apex, lapping at me hungrily as his hands gripped my hips, driving them towards his waiting mouth. He licked up my heat, stopping at my clit and taking it between his lips, sucking hard. Teddy's fingers dug into my flesh, hard enough to bruise. One hand slipped between my legs, and he shoved two fingers into my greedy cunt.

I writhed against his touch and his mouth, clutching his hair as he devoured me. My hips bucked in time with his fingers as they plunged inside me. I cried out as my pleasure took over me. I felt the familiar urge deep in my core, and before I had time to warn him, my pussy erupted and covered him in my pleasure. I couldn't help but giggle as he drowned in my arousal. *Good boy.*

Teddy pulled his mouth from me, a wicked smile took over his glistening face as he breathed, "My fucking God, she squirts. Oh, Peach, you're so wet. So *perfect.*" He moaned, licking up my centre one last time before his eyes darkened and he stood, letting his tall frame loom over me.

"Now, show me how pretty that mouth looks wrapped around my cock."

SEVEN

Jonas

The sound of the back door slamming made me do a double take as I closed the gate to the main paddock. I finished up feeding the animals and turned to head back inside, walking past River's Mini Cooper parked in the driveway. The rear passenger door was wide open with her luggage still on the seat and— *what the fuck was that?*

I walked closer to inspect the object laying in the dirt next to it. A belt. Not just any belt. Teddy's belt. *For fuck's sake.*

I quietly slipped back into the house, bringing her bags with me and being careful not to draw attention to myself. She'd only been here a couple hours, and he'd already sunk his hooks into her. Surely there was some kind of HR rule about fucking your new boss hours after meeting her. Even if there was, Teddy would find a loophole; he always did in these situations.

Creeping up the stairs, I could hear her giggles ringing down the hallway. I followed the sound to his room. The door wasn't closed properly, so I had a perfect view of River and Teddy. Her perched on the bed, on all fours, completely naked and at his mercy. Teddy stood in front of her, gripping her hair as he thrust into her waiting mouth.

My eyes trailed up her body, soaking in the layers of ink that covered her hips, back and shoulders until I reached Teddy's hands. His moans echoed through the room, and I watched as he flung his head back. His eyes rolled back as he found the back of her throat. Tiny beads of sweat dripped down his chiselled body as he plunged into her. Those two together were a work of art.

I felt my dick stiffen in my jeans as I watched her take his cock. Her own hands rubbed against her greedy cunt as she took his length in her mouth. As she sucked him down and pleasured herself, I watched her own cum squirt from her pussy and cover her milky thighs with her release.

She pulled her mouth from Teddy's length, coming up for air. She begged him to fuck her. Teddy released a hand from her hair and bought it down across her dimpled cheek. He rubbed the place where his hand marked her, smirking as he groaned, "Whores are for using, Peach." Then his eyes rolled to the back of his skull as he forced his cock back down her throat.

My cock ached as I watched them together. With Teddy's muscular physique on full display, he looked almost primal as he fucked her mouth. Hand-sized bruises had started forming on her thighs, which means he's already tasted her, and she looked fucking delicious.

I leant against the wooden frame of his door, letting my hand unfasten my belt. I unbuckled my jeans and gripped my cock. I picked up the pace, working my dick frantically as I stood in awe of the scene playing out in front of me. I pictured her throbbing cunt. Her tight little ass begging to be filled. The thought of taking her most forbidden entrance nearly made me come right then and there. They looked so fucking good together.

Teddy ripped his cock from her mouth, precum leaking from his tip. Taking long, slow strides, he walked around the edge of the bed and positioned himself behind her. Still standing he brought his hand down in a firm slap across her plump ass. A beautiful squeal erupted from her smiling, swollen lips. He wrapped her hair in his fists and shoved her forward until her elbows rested against the thick, emerald quilt that adorned his bed.

With another firm slap to her ass, he spat into her back entrance and plunged his thumb into the puckered hole. Driving his cock deep into her greedy pussy, he moaned loudly as he thrust deeper into her. Another delicious squeal seeped from her lips, and she shuddered as he pumped into her.

She bucked furiously against him, and he met her rhythm with his thumb wedged in her ass like an anchor point for stability. They moved together in perfect synchronicity; their bodies entwined as one. I spat down onto my own aching cock, still working myself as I watched them. She screamed his name and several profanities as that sweet gush rushed from her pussy, drenching Teddy's cock with her arousal. He bent forward, letting go of her hair and cupping one breast with his hand. The other pulled away from her back entrance before crashing down in another firm slap across her ass. The instant redness flushed across her ivory skin, and his thrusts deepened, becoming more violent. I could tell he was close. *Good boy.*

The more I watched him fuck her, the more I realised how fucking *good* he looked. His skin was a deep tan from the hours we spent working in the blazing heat. His muscles were toned and full from years of farmwork. Droplets of sweat slid down his stomach and across his abs, where they met in a deep, delicious V above his dick. The way his hips met his ass in a subtle, but definite dip. A soft trail of hair crept up from his groin, resting just shy of his navel. His ass was firm and flexed as he thrust himself into her dripping cunt. I worked my cock harder, faster. I needed *more*. I needed *them*.

Teddy's thrusts became frantic, and River met his pace, still bucking against him wildly. Her back arched against him as he gripped her firmly, pounding into her.

"Teddy, fuck yes!" she screamed.

With one final pump, they came together, completely spent, and I found my own release at the sight of them. The sweet sounds of pleasure dripping from their mouths made me crazy.

I stood for a moment, basking in my post-orgasm glow before realising that I was lurking in the doorway of the dude who is basically my brother. And I just watched him fuck our new landlord. Which is obviously the best moment to rub one out... *Fuck's sake, Jonas, get it together.*

Eight

Teddy

I helped River back into her skirt – such a good, fucking girl. I knew those pretty, tattooed hands would look glorious wrapped around my dick. Her lips were bruised and swollen from taking me, and it was *beautiful*. She gathered the rest of her clothes, pressing a gentle kiss to my cheek as she finished dressing, then turned to leave. She'd barely made it 3 metres when a sudden crash erupted through the house, followed by a huge crack of lightning, and then it was dark.

"Ahhh, what the fuck?" came her high-pitched scream.

"It's okay, Peach, the generator should kick in soon."

"Uhhh... Teddy?" Jonas's familiar, gravelly voice echoed faintly from somewhere outside my room.

"What?"

"The generator is at Mick's. We were supposed to pick it up tomorrow."

"Wait, what does that mean?" River asked, whimpering.

"It means, Amy Pond, that you're about to camp out, mountain style." I made no effort to hide the amusement in my voice as I turned towards my dresser to get a flashlight.

"Amy Pond? Really? We're stranded here with no power, and you're making DR WHO JOKES?" she screamed.

"Yeah, cause your name is River. It's brilliant," Jonas chuckled.

"Calm down, sweet girl," I said, flicking the flashlight on and illuminating her delicious thighs. Judging by the look on her face, I was pretty sure the orgasms I just gave her would not be enough to avoid being murdered brutally in my sleep tonight.

The last few hours had completely escaped me at this point. Although I longed to be inside her again, River and her sweet pussy were the last thing on my mind right now. Jonas and I switched to autopilot, working in tandem to lay out candles. Together, we worked tirelessly to make sure we always had supplies in case we got a big storm. The farm was old, so we had to take care of her; if we didn't take precautions, we'd lose everything. One of the downfalls of living so close to the mountain, I guess. We either missed the storms completely, or they hit us with everything they had. The weather out here can get weird. I often compare it to a Chestnut mare; wild, unpredictable, and ruthless as hell.

Jonas swapped his trademark Akubra for a headlamp. He threw mine to me, and we headed out into the storm, leaving River in my room with the torch. It sucked, because I definitely wanted to stay there with her, but we had to make sure the fences and gates were intact. We couldn't risk losing any stock since we had a sale in a few days. The solar powered flood lights were on, so we were off to a better start than last time...

I checked the main stables and rounded up Alex to make sure our old boy was inside tonight – can't have him out here in this storm. I found him in his usual spot, next to Frank's tractor, as always. He slowed down a lot when Jonas's parents died. They were by far, the best people I had ever met. I still kicked myself when I thought of how lucky I was to have been welcomed into their family. My accident was a huge blow to my plans, but it brought me to the Carters. To Jonas...

"Teddy, we got a post down," came Jonas's voice from the nearby stockyard.

I turned on my heels with Alex close behind, and we followed Jonas's boot prints in the mud towards his voice. He'd already started securing the post when we arrived. I just needed to fill the hole with more dirt to keep it steady 'til morning, when we could check on the damage properly.

"Thank fuck it's only the feed shed, hey?" I laughed, slapping him on the shoulder as we headed back to the house.

NINE

Teddy

Jonas, Alex and I came waltzing in over an hour later, completely soaked and covered in mud. River ran to us, gripping us both in a bear hug, and exhaled so deeply I thought her lungs were going to implode.

"You should have waited for me!" she yelled.

"For what? To slow us down?" I quipped, retrieving our glasses from earlier and topping us up, again.

"Be nice, she doesn't need to take shit from you after what she did for you earlier," Jonas replied. No sooner had the words left his mouth, his eyes widened in panic.

"Pardon me? What do you mean *earlier*?" River asked.

"Nothing, don't worry." Jonas replied, trying to avoid the conversation.

"Jonas?" she demanded, her voice raising as she questioned the man in front of us.

Her eyes narrowed into thin, angry slits as she turned to stare daggers at me.

"Wasn't me, Peach. You watched me fuck her, Jonas?" I interjected, my cock twitching in my jeans.

Come on Jonas, let's play.

"No. I didn't... I don't... I—" he stammered.

I closed the gap between us, staring into his eyes. A feral, hungry rage burned in my own as I moved closer to him.

"Admit it, *brother*. You *love* to watch. You watched me fuck her. You watched her take *my* cock. You watched her cry and beg for *me*. You watched me stretch her and use her. You watched as I filled her pretty, pink cunt with cum. You watched *me*, and you fucking loved it."

Am I really doing this?

"You aren't my brother; you're a fucking idiot. I am so sick of your shit!" Jonas bellowed, his chest rising and falling viciously. The bulge in his pants grew with each breath as I invaded his space. The flickering candlelight barely illuminated the room, but I could feel the tension rising in the air.

Good boy, Jonas. I know you loved it. You've always watched me. Tonight, with River. 14 years ago, with the buckle bunny in the barn. You want me just as much as I want you, don't you?

"I am so fucking glad I am not your brother, Jonas," I replied, lust coating my every word. I peeled the headlamp from his head and stroked my calloused palm through his hair. "Because if I was, it would make what I'm going to do to you so. Much. Worse," I enunciated slowly.

Fuck it.

I gripped Jonas's hair firmly in my hand as I lunged for his mouth. We crashed together, hungrily, roughly. Jonas moaned as I forced my tongue between his lips. His body felt so good against me. His skin warm and slick with rainwater. The way his lips tasted; I had dreamt of tasting those lips for years.

"I hate you," Jonas groaned.

Intense heat dripped from us as we moved together in a delicious frenzy, I almost forgot River was still watching. Our hands roamed each other's bodies, peeling off soaked layers of clothes. His calloused palms felt so unfamiliar, but so right. How he swirled himself around me, our tongues entwining as he deepened our kiss. There was a desperate need between us. It felt like our souls were connecting through our bodies.

Lightning cracked outside, and the sound of thunder bellowed through the house. My heart fluttered as I exposed Jonas's bare chest, which was covered in goosebumps. *Beautiful.* Jonas's jeans hit the floor with a loud, wet thud as he reached for my zipper.

"Good, fuck me like you hate me," I whispered, yanking at his jeans until we stood face-to-face in our underwear, staring at each other. Blind rage and lust crept over Jonas's expressions in the shadows of the dimly lit room.

"Wait, no. I have a better idea." I stopped for a moment, turning to look at River. A puzzled look washed over her face just as I smiled devilishly and said, "Fuck *her* like you hate me."

Ten

Jonas

Teddy's breath smelt like whiskey and cigarettes as he closed the gap between us and flashed me his wicked smile. His rough hands roamed my body; they felt so unfamiliar, but so fucking good. His mouth was warm and inviting. His tongue plunged into me as he deepened our kiss. God, I wanted this. I wanted him. I'd always wanted him.

"Fuck her like you hate me."

Rivers' eyes flashed wide as she registered the words spilling from Teddy's mouth. His face remained completely serious. Teddy reached for her hands, taking them into his own. He placed gentle kisses across the tendrils of ink that covered her knuckles.

"I don't know..." she murmured softly, biting her perfect, pink lips. But the soft twitch at the corner of her mouth told me she did know, and she was very willing. Teddy guided her hands to my chest, assisting her in sliding them down my body, towards my achingly hard cock. Her fingers felt so soft as they gently slid over my skin. I felt so vulnerable, so exposed. Yet somehow, it was fucking bliss.

"Hmmm... Good girl, Peach," he growled, moving himself behind her. He nestled his mouth into the curve of her tattooed shoulder. His tongue slipped from his mouth, tracing the soft lines of ink etched into her neck, until he reached her delicate earlobe and sucked. A gentle moan escaped her lips. Her hands remained fixed above the waistband of my underwear. I could feel her eyes wandering across the throbbing bulge beneath her. She smelt like vanilla and citrus with a delicious, musky finish. I bet she tasted even better.

"Can I kiss you, Red?" My voice was shaky, but it's all I had.

"Red, hey?" she questioned. A cheeky smirk danced on her face as she raised one perfectly shaped eyebrow playfully and winked at me.

"Fucking, come here," I growled, my fingers plunging into her hair. She was so fucking beautiful. I pulled her lips to mine and kissed her hard and deep. Our mouths moved in perfect harmony. I felt her hands find their way underneath my waistband and gently wrap around my pulsating erection. God, her touch felt so good. I hadn't been with anyone in so long that just the friction of her touching my cock and the taste of her lips was enough to send me over the edge. Get it together, Jonas.

"Come on you two. Upstairs. Now," Teddy demanded, gesturing towards the door leading to the staircase.

ELEVEN

Teddy

I slid my hand into River's, her palms felt so delicate compared to Jonas's. She took his hand as I grabbed the flashlight from the bench and led them upstairs to the main suite that we didn't use on a regular basis. I liked this room. It had the California King that I had imported for when I had *house guests,* and the 4-person spa bath that I had installed in the ensuite.

As we slowly entered the bedroom, I could feel River's fingers trembling in mine. *My little Peach was nervous.* The flashlight provided enough visibility for me to see the need in her delicious, honey-coloured eyes. I let go of her hand and made my way around the room in silence, lighting candles and burning an incense stick. Tendrils of scented smoke rose from the dresser and wafted through the room.

They both stood in front of me; a mixture of arousal, fear and intrigue coated their faces as they held each other's hand, waiting for me to speak.

"I want you," I stated.

"Who are you talking to?" River questioned, her voice shaking with uncertainty.

I closed my eyes, inhaled, and let my hands release from the clenched fists they'd been in. I let the exhale escape my mouth before opening my eyes and meeting their gaze. I took one, large step forward, and extended both hands to them.

"Oh, Peach, don't be so naïve… I want you both. I want every single inch of you," I stated slowly as I stalked towards them, picking up both of their free hands. "I want to feel your soft skin as you kiss him. I want to taste your sweet cunt as my brother fucks you. I want to watch you take his cock while I bury mine into him. I want to fuck you both, and I will."

Their jaws damn near hit the floor.

Jonas released her hand and stammered, "I don't know if I… I… I've never…"

I moved closer to him, dropping his hand and pressing mine to his face. Bringing our foreheads together, I whispered— no, I pleaded, "I need you, Jonas. Let me show you. Let me *love* you." My cock throbbed, twitching as I bared my soul to him.

"Teddy, Jonas, I, uh…" River's shaky reply seeped from her pink lips as she stood there, trembling.

"River, my sweet Peach. Let us worship you." I squeezed her hand and pulled her closer to us.

Jonas peeled himself from me, and they met each other's eyes as if seeking their permission and consent. It was like they had developed some sort of unspoken bond in the short time she'd been here. As if they had answered each other internally, they both squeezed my hands and leant in to kiss each other. *There you go.*

"Good girl, little River," I whispered. I pulled her from Jonas and led her into the bathroom, Jonas following close behind us. I turned on the bath tap, and as the water heated up, I added an assortment of salts and soaks as it slowly filled.

I lit and scattered candles while Jonas took his time removing River's clothes. Layer by layer he peeled each item from her, soaking in her flesh as he went. Her body quivered with every touch. After what felt like an eternity of being lost in the sight of her, Jonas got to work on removing both of our underwear. The three of us stood there, naked and silent in the ensuite. I closed the small gap between us, my hands finding each of their waists as I pulled us closer together. Their chests rose heavily as their hearts beat in unison. The two sets of eyes lingering before me danced with lust as they let themselves drift into a state of euphoria with me.

In the faint light of the candles, I admired the art that cascaded across River's body. The intricacy of the mandala work that coated her right arm, trailing its way to the stars that were scattered across her thumb. The gentle flicker of her nipple ring glistening in the dimly lit room. I had been so wrapped up in them, I had forgotten how fucking dark it was.

I glided my hand across River's back, sliding it up her neck and into her hair. I gripped her face with my other hand and pulled her lips to mine. There was nothing delicate about this kiss, it was hard and deep. I was *claiming* her.

I felt Jonas's dick stiffen against my hip as I forced my tongue between River's lips. I let the hand I had resting on Jonas's thigh find its way down to his throbbing erection. *Fuck, he was big*. My mouth watered as I kissed her. My hand gripped her hair while the other worked his cock and I'm pretty sure this is what Heaven feels like.

I pulled my lips from hers, my hand still firmly gripping her hair as I pushed them together. "Good girl, show him how bad you need us," I breathed.

I assumed her greedy cunt was dripping for us by now, so I dropped to my knees, letting my tongue lead the way as I plunged it deep into her. She groaned loudly against Jonas's mouth, her hips grinding against my face wildly. Jonas kissed her with the hunger of a starved man, and he gripped my hair in his hands, driving me deeper into River's sweet, wet pussy.

"Oh, God, Teddy, yes," she screamed, breaking the kiss as she held onto Jonas for stability. Her body convulsed for me, grinding her dripping cunt onto my waiting mouth.

"That's it, Red. Ride his face. You're so fucking perfect, baby," Jonas crooned. He bent down to lavish her perky tits, taking one in his mouth and sucking on her pierced nipple. His other hand reached for her other nipple, and he pinched down. The surreal sensation of pleasure rippled through her as she bucked her cunt against me and screamed our names. *Good fucking whore. My whore.*

A delicious rush of arousal coated my face as her release gushed from her pussy. Her legs gave out and she collapsed into Jonas's ready arms. He held her softly, gently stroking the hair from her face. We helped her climb into the gigantic bathtub, watching desperately as she eased herself in and made herself comfortable. Her delicious curves were completely lost in the mountain of bubbles.

"Your turn, baby," I grinned at Jonas wickedly, lunging for him as our mouths crashed together. I forced her cum from my tongue and into his mouth. My hands instinctively gripped his cock, and then my own. Our lengths rubbed together as my hands worked us in unison. The feeling of his dick pressing against my own as I stroked him was fucking incredible. Our tongues swirled together in a perfect melody and his beard felt so good against my own shaved face.

He moaned into me as I kissed him. But I couldn't help myself, I had to trail kisses down his muscular physique until his cock pulsated against my own greedy mouth.

"Are you ready, baby?" I asked, looking up at him.

"I'm nervous." His lip quivered slightly as he confessed.

"Don't be nervous, Jonas. Let me make you feel good. Let me *do this for you, baby,*" I murmured against his huge, throbbing cock. *God, I was so ready for him. I wanted to own him.*

He gazed down at me, sliding his hands over my face until they met at the back of my skull. A wicked smile came over his gorgeous fucking face as the switch inside him flipped. *Good boy.*

His eyes darkened as he gripped my hair in his fist and snarled, "Be a good little cock tease, and take it all." No sooner had the words filled the room, than he was forcing himself deep into my waiting mouth. *Yes, Sir.*

I gagged on his length as he thrust deeper into me. Tears welling in my ducts. This wasn't the first time I had been with a man, so giving a blowjob wasn't new for me. But nobody had been as big as Jonas and fuuuck, I didn't know it could feel this good having him in my mouth. His calloused hands held my face steady so he could use me how he wanted. I could *just* see River touching herself in the tub. Audible moans seeped from her filthy mouth. My *little Peach liked to watch, hey? Greedy whore.*

Jonas brutally fucked my face, screaming and panting my name repeatedly. His beautiful cock reached further into the back of my throat as he fucked me harder. He soon found his release and warm, salty cum poured down my throat. He held me there as he spent all his seed into me. I felt his body slump as he exhaled, sliding himself out of me with a sigh. He stood still for a moment, our eyes meeting with an intensity that I wasn't used to.

As I swallowed him, I felt his warm, rough hand find my face. Gently stroking the line of my jaw, he pulled my lips up to his and kissed me deeply – tasting himself on my tongue. His kiss was hungry and passionate, like he was claiming me as his own.

"You two are so beautiful together," River whimpered, beckoning us to join her in the water. Her hips ground against the floor of the bath while her tattooed fingers rubbed delicate circles across her clit. *That's my good girl.*

TWELVE
River

Teddy shampooed my hair, placing tender kisses against my shoulders as he rinsed my hair before massaging my scalp as he worked conditioner through my strands. Jonas's hands stroked up my calves playfully. I let myself soak into the bubbles, completely wrapped up in the boys. They made me feel so... safe. The bath water had gone cold quite some time ago, but we didn't move or make any effort to leave. This bath was so big, it was basically a pool.

We cuddled up, laughing, telling stories and learning about each other. We took turns washing each other's bodies, discovering each other. The boys told me more about the history of the farm. Jonas explained how he grew up here – smiling as he spoke of his late parents.

"The old owner was a prick. He never cared, never helped, just threw money at Dad whenever shit broke down. I'm glad he sold the place, plus, the new owner is much prettier," he said with a playful smile.

I was told what a typical day looked like, from clearing the stables to checking the boundary lines. I made a mental note to buy a pair of boots. And a hat. I would like my own hat. Teddy told me they had a horse for me, and he'd take me to meet her once day broke. Her name was Scout. I'd taken riding lessons as a kid, but it'd been years since I'd ridden.

The way their eyes lit up as they talked about the farm – our farm – and the animals that resided here, was so unbelievably sexy. They were so in sync, like an extension of each other. Had they been together before? It didn't seem like it, but surely, they couldn't be this connected if they hadn't? Could they? Watching them together made butterflies erupt in my belly and heat pool in my core.

Teddy chimed in occasionally with a funny story from when they were teenagers. I stroked my hands lazily across them as they spoke, their skin warm and pebbled from the water.

"Jonas here has a bit of a voyeurism kink," Teddy stated, a devious look flashing in his eyes.

"What the fuck are you on about?" Jonas asked. His brows narrowed, forming deep lines above his nose.

"I know you saw me in the barn that day. With the buckle bunny, whatever her name was. She wanted you, but you were so oblivious. I couldn't pass up the opportunity."

Surprise washed over Jonas's face at the admission. "Oblivious? Did you ever think that I just didn't care about any of them because they weren't you?"

Teddy's eyes twinkled, the curves of his full lips creeping into a smirk. "They weren't me?" he asked, his voice shaking nervously.

"No. They were never going to be you," Jonas affirmed.

He slid his hands from my hair, reaching them towards Teddy. They both leaned in, each resting a hand on my thighs as they pressed a gentle kiss to each other's lips. I watched the simple, but intimate confession linger and I felt like I was witnessing two souls colliding. They let their foreheads rest together for a moment before Jonas pulled away, clearing his throat.

"Alright, Red, it's freezing. Let's get you warmed up and in bed. We have a big day tomorrow," he announced. They both got up and helped me from the bath. Jonas carried me bridal style into the bedroom with a stupid, satisfied grin on his face. He started drying me with a towel that felt like a fluffy cloud, while Teddy fetched robes from the dresser.

"I am going to get a bottle from downstairs, don't have too much fun without me." Teddy winked at us as he left the room – leaving Jonas and I alone.

"I'm glad you're here," Jonas smiled at me, and stroked my damp hair as he kissed my forehead. He reached for the dresser and pulled a bottle of lube and massage oil from the top drawer. A wicked smile crept over his face, and he cocked an eyebrow playfully.

"Come here, sweet girl," he said, as he pulled me towards him and kissed me gently. He rubbed the oil into my shoulders, trailing soft kisses across my neck as he worked his strong hands into my aching muscles. When he was finished, I plonked onto the bed with an audible sigh and wiggled my eyebrows at Jonas.

Before he could react, Teddy returned from downstairs with two bottles of red wine balanced in one hand and a cigarette hanging from his full lips.

"And what do you two think you're doing?" he asked, joining me on the bed and passing the cigarette to Jonas.

"Just warming our girl up," Jonas smirked.

"Our girl? What makes you think I want to share you?" Teddy asked wickedly as he popped the cork out of the first bottle of wine.

Jonas leant in seemingly about to kiss Teddy, but instead, slid the cigarette between his lips and turned to look at me. Teddy flashed an equally wicked smile in my direction and pressed his hands to my face, studying me with a feral look in his eyes.

"Can I ask you something?" My eyes never left Teddy's.

"Anything, Peach." He stroked a strand of hair from my face while Jonas edged closer to us, placing his hands on my thighs and leaning into my space. Their eyes softened as they waited for my question.

"You two... have you never...?"

Jonas laughed and kissed the curve of my shoulder before saying, "I have never been with a man before, no. It's been years since I have been with a woman to be honest, Red. I've seen Teddy bring guests over, and I can't say I haven't had opportunities. I guess I was just happy on my own. For a while at least."

"So, why now?" I asked.

Teddy stroked the hair from my face with a sigh as he said, "I don't know. Truly, I don't. I have always been attracted to men and to Jonas, but I never thought we'd act on it. Don't get me wrong, I thought about it, constantly." He chuckled to himself as if recounting a memory of a time where he did just that.

"Seeing you two together, I wanted more. I needed more. I watched you suck his cock. You took him so well, and he looked so fucking gorgeous thrusting into your pretty little mouth. It made me want to be the one he was thrusting into," Jonas offered as he pushed the butt of the cigarette into the ashtray on the dresser.

"You think I'm gorgeous, hey?" Teddy smirked, leaning into Jonas and placing a hand against his rough, bearded cheek. They breathed deeply into each other, their mouths crashing together like angry waves as they kissed. Together, in the subtle candlelight of the room, they looked like works of art.

Tangled in each other next to me, Jonas lunged forward, pressing Teddy into the bed as he reached for me and pulled me into Teddy's chest. Teddy peeled his mouth from Jonas's and met mine, our tongues swirling together furiously.

Jonas trailed kisses down our bodies, his hands roaming our skin as the three of us kissed and caressed each other. I couldn't tell where my body ended and theirs started. We were so close and wrapped in each other. We were like one fluid person.

Jonas smiled as he nervously reached for Teddy's erection, slowly stroking his length as he guided him into his waiting mouth. Teddy quivered and groaned against my kiss as his cock plunged into Jonas, his hips bucking gently as he pressed himself deeper.

"Fuck yes, baby," Teddy growled, gripping my hair while he thrust himself into Jonas.

"Good boys. You like, that don't you?" I murmured into Teddy, nibbling his earlobe and trailing my hand down his chiselled body. I curled my fingers in Jonas's hair and angled him to take Teddy's cock deeper. My pussy was dripping at the sight of the men laid beneath me as they found their pleasure in each other.

"Come here, Peach. Sit on my face," Teddy demanded roughly, pulling me in and gripping my hips to guide me onto him.

I moaned as I rubbed myself against his mouth, his smooth skin soft and warm against my throbbing cunt. His tongue roamed my centre hungrily as he nestled into me, feasting on me like his death row meal. He groaned into my apex as Jonas sucked him down. Intoxicating vibrations ripped through my core, bringing me closer to my release.

I heard a loud pop as Jonas pulled his mouth from Teddy's hard length. Breathlessly standing, his rough hands reached for me as his mouth met my shoulder. His teeth hungrily grazed the sensitive flesh as he sunk his mouth into the curve of my neck. I shuddered in response, breathy moans seeping from my lips.

"Take me Jonas, please," Teddy whimpered against my pussy. His tongue still swirled across my aching clit as he sucked the sensitive bundle of nerves between his lips.

Jonas pressed himself against me, his huge cock was hard and pulsating as he bit down into my neck. He held me down on Teddy's face and reached for the bottle of lube that had been hastily discarded on the bed.

"Turn around, Red. I want you to watch us," Jonas demanded, his voice thick with lust.

Jonas's hands kept me steady as I swirled my hips and lifted myself from Teddy's mouth, turning to face him. Kissing Jonas deeply, I repositioned myself and guided my centre back to Teddy's waiting mouth. His tongue slid across my rear entrance, and I writhed against my men as Teddy's tongue slipped into my opening. My cunt throbbed painfully over his chiselled jaw as he furiously took my ass. The sensation of his tongue inside me was fucking euphoric.

Jonas sucked my pierced nipple between his lips, and the warmth of his mouth on my sensitive area had me in a frenzy. He squirted the lube onto his dick, working himself as I fucked Teddy's face. His lube covered hand met Teddy's cock, and he stroked them both. A satisfied smile pulled across his face as he watched us find our pleasure together.

"Are you ready, baby?" he asked.

Teddy came up for air and whimpered against my centre, "God, yes. I need you, Jonas."

Jonas bit his bottom lip, guiding his cock to Teddy's opening. Jonas held his breath as he pushed his cock gently inside Teddy, grunting as he met the resistance of his tight hole. Both men groaned loudly as Jonas eased himself deeper into Teddy – one hand firmly on his hip, the other holding his cock for stability. Teddy quivered beneath me, breathing deeply as Jonas entered him. The shaking caused an overwhelming feeling of heat low in my belly.

"Fuck yes, Jonas. You're so fucking big," Teddy moaned, returning his mouth to my pussy and completely devouring me. His tongue swirled against me, and he sucked my clit with gentle nips. Jonas found his rhythm, thrusting himself into Teddy with long, slow strokes as he moaned our names.

My hips bucked furiously against Teddy's face. The sight of these men fucking each other made my cunt clamp down onto Teddy's tongue as I rode him. I was feral for these men. I screamed their names, riding Teddy into oblivion as he took Jonas deep inside him. They looked so fucking perfect.

I leant forward slightly and wrapped my hand around Teddy's thick cock. I returned my pleasure to him, working his dick in time with Jonas's thrust as he devoured my pussy and took Jonas so well in his ass.

My pleasure ripped through my body as I moaned. "Good boy Teddy, take him, baby. You look so beautiful."

The sensation of being so wrapped up in these men was absolutely intoxicating. My own orgasm was building in my core, and I was ready to explode for them.

"I'm so fucking close," Jonas grunted, pinching my breast and kissing me hard as he plunged himself deeper into Teddy.

"Me too, baby. Harder, please!" Teddy begged. His eyes rolled back in his head as he crept closer to the edge of nirvana.

One final thrust and they found their release together – Teddy spending himself over my hand and onto his stomach, as Jonas emptied himself inside Teddy's ass. My pace slowed and I lifted myself from Teddy's face, letting my boys bask in their post-orgasm bubble. They both smiled at me, then at each other, completely satiated. Jonas slowly pulled himself from Teddy, and they collapsed on the bed, wrapping their legs together.

"Come here, Peach." Teddy patted the space between them, beckoning me to join them. I curled up between the boys and they draped their arms across my body. They each trailed their fingers across my skin, as goosebumps covered the places that felt their touch.

"River?" Jonas whispered.

"Yeah?" I replied.

"Thank you."

My eyebrows arched as I flashed him a puzzled look. "For what?"

"For making me feel like I'm not some weirdo who got off on watching my brother fuck our landlord, and that exploring new things is okay, even if it's different or new. I guess I have always felt sort of... alone?"

"Well, you are a weirdo who got off on watching your brother fuck the landlord," Teddy butted in and laughed. "But I love that you're getting all mushy since I made you see stars."

"Fuck off, asshat. I'm pretty sure I just made you see stars," Jonas laughed in reply.

"He's right though, Peach. You're something else," Teddy said, smiling softly as his eyes closed. He leant in and kissed me gently, murmuring sweet nothings against my lips.

We cuddled up in bed together. One man on either side of me, yet both draped across me comfortably. Even in the dimly lit room, I could make out Jonas's fingers carefully tracing my tattoos long after our conversation gradually lulled. I laid there quietly, feeling every stroke of Jonas's touch. I felt comforted by the sounds of their soft breaths, and their heartbeats slowing to a gentle, steady rhythm as they fell asleep.

Was this a one-time thing?

Would we talk about this tomorrow?

Were we all together now?

I had no idea what tomorrow would bring, but at that moment, I felt safe. I felt happy. I felt home.

THIRTEEN

Jonas

s I laid in bed with them, my legs wrapped around Rivers' and tangled in the sheets, with Teddy's hand lazily resting over her stomach and stroking my arm, I felt *warm*. This woman had been here about 10 hours, and she'd unravelled layers of me that I didn't even know existed. Teddy placed slow, gentle strokes through her auburn hair - the hint of a smirk dancing across his mouth.

I loved watching her with Teddy; the way her body fit perfectly with his. I loved watching her ride his face as I fucked him. *God, he felt so good.* I had always liked anal play, but I never thought I would like fucking a *man* so much. I watched Teddy's eyes flicker as he fell asleep; he looked so peaceful curled up next to our girl. That's what she was now: *ours.* She was *perfect,* and I knew at that moment that I was never letting her go.

I was content with whatever this was, and whatever it would be. I suppose that's something we'd have to work out at some point. For now, I just wanted to exist here with them. I felt their skin lazily pressed against mine and allowed myself to soak in the feeling of comfort that came with being here with them. River's eyes slowly fluttered as she drifted off, and her soft whimpers sent a rush of blood to my dick.

Did this mean I was bi?

Did it even matter?

I laid awake for what felt like an eternity, replaying scenarios over and over in my head as I watched them sleep. I trailed my hands across the intricate flowers that surrounded the large fox etched across the centre of River's back. Three butterflies sat neatly next to it, caressing her shoulder blade. Small stars filled the gaps between the inked art. The tendrils of ink cascaded across her left arm in dark florals that stopped just shy of her elbow. Two ropes of barbed wire wrapped around her forearm, the swirls of line-work coating her fingers.

She shivered against my touch as I traced my fingers lightly across the outline of the detailed mandala art lining her right arm. I stopped as I reached the constellation of stars scattered across her thumb and wrapped my hand over hers. My eyes felt heavy and as they met the darkness, I let sleep wash over me.

FOURTEEN
Jonas

12 years ago. Age 21

I hastily flung the bridle onto the bench in the shed, and turned on my heels, storming out into the paddock towards the house, when I noticed the gate to the stable nearby was wide open. *Strange... I swear I closed it.*

I changed my direction, my pace quickening as I neared the open gate. I was within touching distance of the stable when I heard faint, feminine giggles echoing from within the walls. *What the fuck?*

I crept closer, peering through the gaps in the chestnut wood. A flash of tanned flesh darted across my vision, accompanied by what appeared to be a pair of Wranglers being flung across the floor.

"Teddy, yes!" the feminine voice panted.

"Turn around and spread that perfect ass for me, baby," the familiar voice of my brother demanded in reply.

I quietly peered closer, allowing my eyes to take in the sight of the woman before me barely hidden by the wooden panels separating us. She smiled as she bent over and bared her round ass to my brother. A thin, white lace bra was half pulled down her chest. Her full breasts spilled from their case, bouncing gently as she pressed her ass back, grinding her cunt against Teddy.

I felt my dick stiffen in my jeans. I hadn't been intimate with anyone before. But ever since Teddy turned 16, he has paraded every second girl in town in and out of his room – so seeing one underneath him now wasn't out of character, although the stable was a change of scenery. I don't know how Mum and Dad never noticed them...

Teddy's dark, flannel shirt slid from his shoulders as he leant forward and trailed kisses down her neck. His hand curled up her spine and met his mouth, gripping her throat firmly as he slapped the other down against her ass. I was in awe of how his muscular frame pressed against her; the way his hands slid over her curves; how his biceps flexed as he lifted her from the hay bale and flipped her to face him; the way his lips curled into a smirk as he knelt before her, inhaling her scent before suctioning his mouth to her glistening entrance; the sound of his moans as he feasted on her. He looked incredible.

My cock ached for friction. It pressed painfully against my jeans, throbbing for release. My hand slid to my erection. I pushed down on my length and rubbed myself over the fabric to quiet the ache. My eyes still lingered on the pair, and I watched in awe as she swallowed him down. Her pretty mouth was so full, so swollen. My cock felt like it was going to burst, and I felt my entire body shiver with anticipation and desire. I raised a hand to lean against the chestnut frames before me, the other still clutching my dick through my jeans. *Creaaak.*

Fuck.

I halted for a moment, waiting to be caught. But as I let my eyes fall back to the pair before me, I was thankful to see them completely preoccupied with each other.

"That's it, baby, open for me," Teddy growled. His cock pulsing as he pulled himself from her cunt and plunged himself into her ass. Her cries of pleasure echoed through the stable as he invaded her tight hole. *My God. They looked incredible.*

His ass was firm and flexed as he thrust into her, beads of sweat formed across his thick brows. His eyes darkened as he groaned and found his pleasure inside her.

I longed to touch him. To touch her. I felt my dick explode in my jeans, looking down to see the mess seeping through the denim. The sound that came from Teddy at that moment was something otherworldly, and he convulsed as the aftershocks of his orgasm ripped through him. He pulled himself from her, stroking her hair with a pleased smile plastered on his face. *I had to get the fuck out of here.*

FIFTEEN

Teddy

Present Day

I would be lying if I said I had never thought about being with Jonas. He was gorgeous, and something about being with a man made me feral. I loved their roughness, how they used me. I had always been a dominant man – especially in bed. The act of letting myself submit to someone felt so *freeing*.

I closed my eyes; my limbs wrapped around the two people beside me. I laid there with them and replayed the events of today in my mind over, and over. How this little vixen showed up and threw a spanner in our mundane routine of kicking around here together alone. Her vibrant energy and playful demeanour were infectious, and I couldn't get enough of her. I loved that she brought Jonas out of his shell and made him feel safe enough to explore himself, and me. I had craved him for years. I never thought that I would be allowed to taste his lips or feel him pressed against me.

The image of River riding my face embedded itself into my mind on a loop. The way her plump ass ground against me as I devoured her greedy cunt. How good Jonas looked as he plunged into my ass, holding onto our girl to stabilise his thrusts. How she worked my dick as she used my mouth. The contrast of the dark, intricate ink on her perfectly manicured hands as it twisted over her porcelain flesh. How fucking good those hands looked wrapped around my cock. She, like her tattoos, were a work of fucking art.

I had been with couples before, but the unspoken connection between these two sent a pool of heat straight to my dick. It was unbelievable. Seeing how they collided together and instinctively found their place with each other. How they were so eager to explore with me.

The fleeting moment of hesitation when I told them I wanted them felt like a distant memory now. We connected like one perfect unit. Well, I hoped that's what we were. I hoped we would wake up and continue our little bubble of happiness. I needed them.

"Goodnight, Peach. Goodnight, Jonas," I murmured softly. My eyes felt heavy, and I drifted into a deep, comfortable sleep.

SIXTEEN

Teddy

10 years ago. Age 20

I stumbled out of the bar towards Jonas's ute. The burn of the whiskey still lingered in my throat. I climbed into the cab, smiling wickedly as I toyed with the scrunched-up napkin in my palm. "What's that?" Jonas asked with a furrowed brow.

"Chick from the bar gave me her number. Reckon she wants me to show her boyfriend a thing or two," I chuckled, sliding into the cab.

Jonas shook his head as a smile creased his jaw. He reached into the console, pulled out a packet of cigarettes, and flicked the top to expose the perfectly wrapped tobacco. I slid one from the packet, easing it between his lips – those fucking lips – before doing the same to my own.

"Thanks for picking me up, bro," I slurred. Then I sparked the tip of his cigarette, lighting my own immediately after and taking a deep inhale.

"Someone's gotta make sure you don't drown yourself in whiskey," he replied.

I felt the bite of air against my cheeks as I rolled down the window and sighed. "I missed you today," I confessed.

"You're the one who stayed in town last night," he said with a shrug.

"Duty called, brother."

"By duty, do you mean Eileen?" He asked.

"Yeah, something like that. Who cares?" My eyes darkened as I questioned my brother. Why did he care? He was always prying into the chicks I brought home. He got even weirder about it the first time I brought a bloke back from the bar.

His smile faded as he continued inhaling the cigarette that hung lazily from his lips. They were a faded, rose-like shade of pink – only slightly concealed by the facial hair he always wore. I reckon I could sink my teeth into those lips and be a happy man.

His deep-brown eyes shone like marbles, and the corners creased into soft lines when he smiled. *Why are you smiling, Jonas? Did you catch me staring?* I sat there in the passenger seat, absorbing the size of him. He was always taller than me, but since he hit his 20s, he sat around 6'3" and would easily clock in at 110 kg of pure *strength*. Light freckles dusted across the tanned skin of his forearms as they peaked out from the rolls of flannel that were bunched up in the crook of his elbow. The sensation of blood rushing to my dick pulled me out of my trance.

I flicked my cigarette into the ashtray, and my hand reached for the open pack in the centre console at the same time Jonas's did. Our fingers brushed against each other, forcing electricity to ignite through us at the feel of his calloused skin against my own. He pulled away rapidly, his brow furrowing as he said, "You zapped me, ya prick!" A deep, velvety laugh exploded from him as he shook his head.

"Sorry, man," I replied.

We continued the drive back home, talking shit about anything and everything. I couldn't shake the feeling that the spark I felt through my body was something else.

Something worse.

Something... forbidden.

Seventeen

Jonas

Present Day

I was up before the Rooster crowed – literally – working on preparing breakfast. The Almighty Alex was still curled up on his dog bed in the lounge room, and the others had yet to surface from our room. *Our room... Too soon?*

I had just fired up the portable grill when a gravelly voice interrupted the silence. I didn't have to look to know who it belonged to, he was awake. *This is it, the moment of truth...*

"Well, good morning to you too, baby." Teddy slowly closed the gap between us, his underwear hanging lazily off his hips, accentuating the line of hair that I knew led straight to his cock.

God he was gorgeous.

His smoky-green eyes danced as he moved closer to me, a devilish grin creeping over his lips. As he leant into my space, it occurred to me that the last time we were in this spot was when he kissed me last night. My thoughts were interrupted as I felt his breath on my tongue as he dipped his chin and pressed his lips to mine. I opened my mouth for him instinctively, my hands reaching for his hips. I needed him *closer*.

"Morning," I murmured with a grin. His hands brushed through my hair as he pulled away from our kiss, smiling at me.

"So… you want some help?" he asked.

"Yeah, can you find some eggs?" I laughed in reply.

I should probably mention now that I cannot cook to save my fucking life. I ate most of my meals at the pub, or whatever casserole-thing Mrs Hartford, our neighbour, dropped us.

Teddy shook his head and laughed as he said, "Why don't we get our girl, go see how the place held up last night, and head into Maverick's? I am sure Hannah's cooking will shit on whatever the fuck you were gonna dish up."

He was right. About both things. We needed to check on the property, and the local diner was well-renowned for its farm-to-table meals. Hannah and her family had been here almost as long as we had. I smiled in agreement and let him take my hand and guide me up the staircase to check on River.

EIGHTEEN

Teddy

It took River forty-five fucking minutes to get her sweet ass out of bed. I didn't complain – given that it took her forty-five minutes because the second we appeared to tell her we were going out she pounced on us like a rabid cat. Her flaming hair cascaded down her neck in ribbons as she squeezed herself into what looked like a brand-new pair of Wranglers.

"Need some help there, Red?" Jonas asked, sparking a cigarette and wiggling his eyebrows.

"No, I'm fine. These are just new jeans, and I need to wear them in," she protested, still wiggling around like a worm.

I slapped her ass and strolled over to Jonas, prying the cigarette from his calloused hands and taking a deep drag. He smirked at me, and we silently shared a moment while we waited for our girl to get her shit together.

As we walked downstairs, slowly making our way to my ute, we could see some of the damage from the storm. Jonas and I did a quick loop on foot of the main yards to make sure nothing was urgent and none of the stock had fallen overnight. Thankfully, all was well – aside from the gigantic fucking tree that had fallen across the driveway.

"Gimme a hand, would ya?" Jonas called. He gestured to River to jump in the driver's seat and warm up the engine while he secured the portable winch to the back of the ute. I wrapped the winch rope around a thick branch, and we talked River through towing the tree across the dirt road it currently obstructed.

"Good job, Red," Jonas smiled. River's golden eyes danced at the praise. *God, she is adorable.* I couldn't wait to teach her how things were done around here. My good girl.

Jonas showed River how to check the fuse box next, while I checked on our makeshift post from last night. Thankfully, it wasn't that bad – the winds were nowhere near as damaging as the last storm we had. The mountains seemed to have protected our little corner of the world... this time.

I met them back by the stables. Alex was trotting along beside them, tucking closely into River's heels – he had really taken a shine to her. I kicked open the barn door, waltzing into the barn to check the horses. Then I saw it. A tiny smear of blood across the nearby stall. Scout's stall. The horse who was meant to be River's. *What the fuck?*

"Jonas! Come here. Look. Blood."

As he hurried to me, the sound that flooded our ears stopped us both in our tracks. That familiar, high-pitched, nicker. *No fucking way.*

Jonas instantly lifted the gate to Scout's stall, and sure as shit, there she was, laying down, looking absolutely exhausted. Her elegant neck arched gently around a dark silhouette. There, laying before us, was a tiny, grey foal nestled cozily in its mother's embrace.

"Oh. My. God," Jonas stammered. He slowly edged forward, entering the stall with his open palm extended to the mare.

"Guess this explains why she's been such a moody bitch," I laughed.

River slapped my arm as she gently walked into the stable to check on Scout.

"Did you know she was in foal?" she asked.

"Not a damn clue. I guess this makes us grandparents," I replied, shaking my head in disbelief.

Jonas stroked Scout's blaze, planting a gentle kiss on her muzzle before turning to exit.

"They both look healthy. We have ourselves a little boy. We'll have to get Hudson out here to check on them, but for now, let's let them get some rest," he said as he strolled out of the stall.

The three of us – and Alex the Almighty – followed him and got to work checking the fences on the boundary line. Thick mud caked across my Ariats as I trudged through the paddock. Jonas was close behind me, and River took the rear with her new sidekick at her feet. The sun beat down against my shoulders, and beads of sweat started forming across my brow. We'd already been out here for a few hours but still had a ways to go. In the haste of cleaning up, we'd completely forgotten about eating. I don't know about the other two, but my stomach was angrily growling at me, and I needed to sink my teeth into one of Hannah's big breakfasts immediately. Breakfast for lunch is always appropriate.

"I'll head back to the house and check on the stock, are you good with the rest of the fences?" Jonas asked, walking toward me down the fence line.

"Yeah, go. Take Peach with you. She can check on Scout and the foal," I replied.

Jonas nodded, removing his Akubra and running a hand through his hair – now damp with sweat. He closed the gap between us, his stance relaxed as he stooped himself lower to meet my height. He was only a few inches taller than me, but his frame was nearly twice the size. I was fit, and muscular, but he was fucking *jacked.*

"Are you bossing me around, Teddy?" he asked with a grin. His brows cocking playfully as he invaded my space.

"So, what if I am?" I questioned him in reply. My breath hitching as he intoxicated my senses. He was so close I could feel his cock twitching in his jeans.

"That isn't a very good idea, baby."

His eyes darkened, and his hands plunged into my hair, as his mouth claimed mine. His kiss was messy. Hungry. Raw. He wasn't being gentle; he was being *fucking powerful.*

He finally broke away. Both of us stood there, breathlessly staring at each other. I looked past him to River, who had casually propped herself against a nearby fencepost and was scratching behind Alex's ear.

"Welcome back to Earth you two," she giggled. Her eyebrows wiggled uncontrollably as she shook her head.

"Don't stop on my account, I'll see *you* back at the house." She pointed to Jonas with a wicked smirk on her face as she turned to leave, Alex hot on her heels. Her footsteps grew quieter, and she disappeared from sight.

Jonas's hands gripped my throat as he brought his face so close to mine that our lips brushed. Only this time, his eyes were dark and deranged, though still glistening behind his thick lashes.

"You wanna see who's boss? Get on your knees," he demanded, the pressure on my throat showing me the direction he wanted me. His dominant side made me absolutely *feral.*

Without hesitation, I did what he said. The opportunity to be at his mercy – be controlled by him – was too good to pass up. He didn't even have to tell me to undo his belt buckle or unzip his jeans. No, that I did all on my own, letting his cock spring from his underwear and in the direction of my face.

Jonas's rough hand moved from my throat, and he brushed my cheek with the back of his knuckles. "Such a good boy for me. Now suck."

And. Suck. I. Did. I needed to please him.

Tiny beads of sweat formed across his brows as he thrust himself into my throat. "God, you feel so. Fucking. Good," he panted with each deep thrust. His cock throbbed as he bottomed out inside me. My hands gripped his muscular ass, feeling him flex with every movement. Tears welled in my eyes. He was so fucking big. So fucking *delicious*.

Jonas ripped his dick from my mouth. His body shook as ribbons of cum released from his cock and coated the ground beneath us. I was about to get up when his hands firmly wrapped around me and pulled me to stand. *God, he was strong.*

His eyes darkened, and it felt like he was devouring me with his glare. "I need you, baby."

My hands instinctively reached for his cock. The messy smear of cum and my saliva coating his length made it so easy to stroke him. The sensation sent a rush of blood to my already hard dick. Even completely spent, the size of him rivalled me.

"I fucking love your cock," I moaned, my breath desperate and needy. Lust fuelled my veins like heroin. I couldn't get enough. I needed to fill this man. I craved the feeling of my cum exploding inside him. I would *beg* for this man to scream my name. Demand he be mine.

I wanted to watch my cum leak from him.

Can you have a breeding kink for another man?

Jonas leant in and kissed me. It was a different kiss than before; it was softer. Familiar. Safe. Where his last kiss was hungry and forceful, this one was almost... delicate.

He slowly put himself away as he leaned out of our kiss. With his forehead pressed to mine he whispered, "I feel like I have waited a lifetime to feel what I feel when I'm with you, Theodore."

"Theodore? 'Sir' will do," I replied with a wink.

"Fucking idiot," he laughed. His smile was just as beautiful as the first time I saw it.

"Let's go," I said. My voice lowered an octave as I detailed my fantasy to the man before me. "If we stay out here any longer, I'm going to bend you over, stuff you with my cock, and fuck you senseless until my cum leaks from you and you beg me to stop."

"I think I would like that. A lot." His cheeks flushed crimson, and I made a mental note to do that later.

I smiled at him, took his hand, and we walked together through the paddocks, back to our girl. I couldn't help but feel grateful she let us have our moment. It would take us some time to find our groove together, but I really felt like we were already on the way to making it work, whatever *it* was. In this moment, as I held my man's hand and we made our way back towards the woman who had unravelled us, I was sure that I would do anything to keep them.

NINETEEN

Jonas

That afternoon, we strolled into Maverick's, side-by-side, an unstoppable unit. We'd been out in the paddocks since daybreak. I was dying for a cold one and a feed. I guided the three of us into the booth at the back where Teddy and I usually sit. River squirmed in her seat as she toyed with the menu that sat lazily on the table.

Teddy and I fooling around on the boundary line was both unexpected and incredible at the same time. Boy had I worked up an appetite, and the image of him on his knees for me was burned into my brain on a loop. It was very distracting.

"Oi, Hannah!" Teddy shouted across the diner. "Tell your good-for-nothin' cousin he sold me a fuckin' broodmare! Scout went into foal during the storm. We've got ourselves a colt!"

Hannah Jensen – along with her trademark blonde curls and cherry lipstick – strolled confidently out from the kitchen. A warm smile radiated across her plump lips as she chuckled, "Mornin', boys! I'll be sure to sort him out for you. Now, who is this gorgeous lady y'all are keepin' all to y'selves?" she asked.

Her thick Southern accent hadn't faded at all, even though she moved to Australia over a decade ago. I found her tone gentle and soothing.

"This is River Carlisle, she bought Ashwood. River, this is Hannah Jensen, she owns Maverick's," I offered, gesturing to the women. Hannah extended her hand to River, and her infectious cherry smile reached River's as the two women shared an unspoken moment.

"Well, River Carlisle. It's mighty fine to meet ya'. Hey, do you like wine?" she asked.

"I am quite partial to a cheeky cabernet," River replied with a slight smirk toying at her lips as she remembered how she got here. *Cheeky girl.*

"Alright, it's settled. You're joining our book club!" Hannah announced.

"Book club?"

Jonas shook his head as he interjected, "By *book club,* she means once a month the ladies have a sleepover here at the diner, get blind drunk, and sing karaoke." Hannah playfully slapped Jonas's arm.

"Oh, shush your mouth, Jonas Carter!" Her sweet, Southern accent thickened as she blushed.

"I would LOVE to join the book club!" River announced proudly, as a satisfied smile crept across her face.

"God help us all." I sighed, pressing a kiss to River's forehead.

Hannah finished sharing the details of the upcoming festivities with River, gave her a run-down of the families in town, and spilled some miscellaneous gossipy information. As she turned to leave our booth, her eyes trailed across Jonas and me. I hadn't noticed that my hand was lazily resting on his knee, but Hannah had. *Of course she had.*

"Anything else y'all wanna tell me, aside from being horse grandparents?" she asked, cocking a brow.

"Jonas tried to cook this morning," I replied with a laugh.

Hannah leaned in closer; her brow still raised in an inquisitive expression as she proudly announced, "There ain't a single person in this town that's gonna be mad about you two being happy – however that looks. Now knock it off and stop hidin' out!" She placed a kiss on both of our cheeks – her signature cherry lipstick now etched across our skin.

"And you, young lady," she said, placing a matching kiss on River's cheek. "You take good damn care of those boys, and they'll take good damn care of you, okay? Welcome to Fires Creek, honey!"

Twenty
River

8 months later

"Hannah, hurry up!" I called from the next room. I swear to God, we were already running late for book club, and she had barely started her makeup.

The boys had *insisted* on accompanying us this evening. They said it was because there was a game on at the diner, but I knew they just wanted an excuse to get out of the manor.

The last few months had been insane. The boys had just finished a huge muster with the cattle and there was another one coming up. Since I couldn't ride confidently yet, I stayed home with Scout and Lenny. Don't ask about the foal's name – Teddy thought it 'matched Uncle Teddy's name.' *Jonas and I both rolled our eyes at that one.*

It only took a couple of days to clean up after the storm; we were actually pretty lucky. The Hartford's copped the brunt of it, so the whole town joined forces to help them out. Brenda and her husband, Alan, were getting on, and there's no way in hell those two could have done it alone.

We had taken shifts and designated areas of the property to make sure everything was cleaned, fixed, and ready for business. Honestly, with the number of volunteers, it only took a few days to return the Hartford Farm to its glory. I hadn't seen it before, but Teddy assured me we'd actually improved the place.

"Can I borrow that little leather skirt thing?" Hannah asked, snapping me out of my daydream. She was still curling her wild blonde hair.

"You mean this one?" I questioned in reply, holding up the skirt I had worn my first day here.

"That's the one! Thanks, darlin! Link's gonna looooove it!"

"Link? The fucking *realtor?*" I exclaimed. "The guy you've been telling me about is LINK?"

"Shhhh! If the boys hear you, they'll never shut up about it!" she retorted.

"Is he not gay?" I asked, my voice rising in pitch slightly.

"River, honey. Surely, by now, *you* would have realised that it's all just a sliding scale when you're attracted to someone. Besides, where do you think your toyboy learned his tricks?" she giggled hysterically.

Teddy chose that exact moment to stride into the room – without knocking – and shoved Hannah's shoulder playfully with his usual devilish smile plastered to his face.

"Miss Jensen, I'll have you recall that you were not concerned by my *tricks* when you were the receiver of them, now were you?" He bowed to her as he placed a kiss against her delicate hands.

I scoffed and continued getting dressed. "Good God, Teddy, is there anyone in this town you haven't fucked?" I asked, throwing a nearby pillow at him to assert my dominance. *It was pink and fluffy. Mission unaccomplished.*

He feigned shock. "Of course there is, Peach!"

"Oh really?" I said, taunting him.

"Our dear neighbours, Brenda and her beloved husband, said no when I asked." His smile was wickedly cheeky as the words came out of his mouth.

He lunged at me, tackling me onto the bed and pinning my hands above my head. I laughed as I instinctively curled my legs around his waist, pressed my lips to his, and kissed him deeply. Our bodies were made for each other. He caught my lower lip between his teeth and bit down on the soft flesh. I could taste his last cigarette that lingered on his tongue as it swirled against mine. I broke away from our kiss, and my eyes lingered gently on his. My hands wrapped lazily around his neck and held his face.

At this point, I was so lost in him that I completely forgot Hannah was still curling her hair several feet away from us.

"Alright!" she announced, stepping into our space. "You two love-birds need a minute, or can we get the cranky one and go?" She wiggled her perfectly sculpted eyebrows towards us before she turned on her heels and headed for the door.

As she left the room, I couldn't help but notice just how beautiful she was. Her height far-surpassed mine. Her hips dipped deeply against her ass, her belly round and soft beneath the waistband of my skirt. Honestly, after seeing her in my clothes, I knew there was no way in hell I could ever wear it again.

"We better go, Peach. If I have my way with you, you won't be all pretty for your book club."

He lifted himself from me, extending his hand to mine and helping me from our bed. As I started walking towards the door, following Hannah downstairs where Jonas was waiting – no doubt a few whiskeys in – Teddy caught my hand and pulled me back. He invaded my space in one fluid motion, pressing me against the doorframe. The feeling of his body against me intensified the heat pooling low in my belly.

"I love you, River," he confessed. "I love every fucking *inch* of you. I love your stupid sense of humour. I love how you see me. See *us*. I love you, and I fucking LOVE your sweet little ass!" He smiled, his cock pressing into me as he ground his hips against my centre. The way we fit together was visceral. We were like an extension of each other – completely connected.

"Do you have to bloody ruin everything?" I squealed, pushing him off me and gesturing to the surprise guest in his jeans.

"Peach?" He said, though it was really more of a question. His voice had dropped to barely a whisper.

"I love you too, Theodore. Always."

TWENTY-ONE
River

I was onto my third glass of Cabernet before Jonas strode up to me with a cheeky smile and whispered against my ear, "Careful, Red. Don't you remember what happened last time you had a few wines?"

Before I could open my mouth to speak, I felt Teddy's presence linger behind me as he joined us. I could smell the lingering scent of tobacco when he nestled his mouth into my neck. "Peach?" he slurred. "Are you being a bad girl?"

"Come on, baby, we better take our seats. Red's up next," Jonas confessed.

"Wait, what?" I asked, confusion lacing my voice.

Jonas didn't have a moment to answer my questions before Link appeared on the make-shift Karaoke stage that we set up for 'Ladies Night' – AKA 'The Book Club', AKA 'Karaoke Night'. His classic *Realtor for the Stars* voice rang through the diner as he announced, "Ladies and Gentlemen of Fires Creek. We have a special treat for you tonight. Please welcome to the stage, River. Fucking. Carlisle!"

Our neighbours and friends erupted in cheers, whistles, and laughter. Before I could comprehend what I just heard, Teddy lifted me from my seat and carried me towards the stage, while Hannah laughed hysterically from her perch on the counter across from me. The sound of my boots echoed against the wooden floor as Teddy dropped me next to Link, who narrowed his eyebrows as he passed me the microphone with a smirk. "Ready, darlin'?"

The bass increased as Hannah turned the music up louder. The familiar intro of 'Bottom's Up' by Brantley Gilbert faded in from the previous song and radiated through my body and the diner. *Of course she picked this song. Bitch.*

I had – in confidence – told her last time we had a girl's night at Ashwood, that I loved this song. I had climbed onto the table, using a spoon as a microphone, and performed the living shit out of it for her. That night ended with her passing out on the couch and Teddy throwing me over his shoulder and carrying me up to bed. Jonas was patiently waiting for us, already naked and hard. *The boys were always starting without me.*

I took a deep breath and let my eyes close, letting the music enter my soul. My body became one with the beat, my hips swirling instinctively to the song. My eyes flashed open, and as the first line of the song amped up from the speakers, so did my inner confidence.

I belted the song – there was no stopping me now. I was drunk, I was happy, and I was completely in my element. The sound of my boys cheering my name only egged me on as I pranced around the platform. I felt every riff, every lyric, every drumbeat. I was living my small-town *Coyote Ugly* fantasy, and nobody could stop me.

The guitar solo started and so did my feet. I didn't hold back. The chorus that followed was sung with passion and fire. As the final beat burst through the diner, I stomped my well-worn boots hard against the floor beneath me, punched my fist into the air, and smiled.

The next song, 'Austin' by Dasha faded in from the speakers before my applause was over. Hannah had made me learn the TikTok line dance, and you bet your sweet ass I was absolutely doing it. I dragged her from her perch on the counter to the middle of the dance floor, and we stomped and twirled our way through every beat – our boots clunking in unison like a sweet melody.

I was loved.

I was home.

I was fucking *invincible*.

That song ended, and the next one erupted from the speakers. Jonas joined us on the dance floor – drink in hand – and wrapped his arm around my waist from behind. He nuzzled his bearded chin into my neck as his hips moved in time with my own.

"You smell so fucking good, Red," he growled against my earlobe. Taking it in his mouth and sucking on the milky flesh. His tongue was warm and wet as he trailed kisses down the column of my neck. His empty hand snaked its way up to my throat and coaxed my head back until our eyes met. The deep-chocolate of his eyes sent pools of heat to my core.

"Open your mouth," he demanded, his eyes burning into mine.

My lips parted and I arched my neck, baring myself to him. He took a swing of his drink, then his lips met mine as he spat the warm, honey bourbon into my mouth. He spun me to face him, the liquid now burning my throat and his tongue encircled mine. His kiss was rough and hard, like he was claiming me.

As I pulled away, his lips crept into a satisfied smile. His tongue slid across the pink flesh, and his eyes closed as bit his lower lip. "Red?"

"Hey," I replied, as I nestled my head into his chest. I felt his lips brush against my hair as he pressed a gentle kiss to the top of my head.

His hand stroked through my locks like he was scared I'd disappear if he didn't hold onto me.

"You smell good," he groaned. I giggled as I looked up, meeting the deep pools of chocolate beneath his lashes.

"I love you, River Carlisle."

"I love you, Jonas Carter."

He had told me he loved me once before, one night as we were moving the cattle in from the stockyard. He wasn't one with words. His love language was more on the acts of service scale.

I had never been cared for the way he cared for me. Little things like washing my hair, polishing my boots, or helping me wash the truck. He was always finding ways to provide for me – and I cherished every moment.

Teddy stumbled out from behind the bar in the diner, holding a bottle in one hand and a cigarette in the other. I felt his hand meet Jonas's against my waist until I was completely surrounded by my men.

"Am I interrupting something?" he slurred.

"Always," I teased.

Jonas took a sip of his whiskey, a cheeky smirk slowly commandeering his mouth. Teddy twirled me around between them, removing his Akubra and placing it lazily atop my head. "Much better, Peach," he observed with a nod of approval. His mouth met mine, the kiss hungry and deliberate.

Jonas's hand guided me closer to Teddy until our hips sat flush, then he ground himself against me. Pools of heat welled in my cunt as the sensation of their skin on mine sent goosebumps across my flesh. I kissed them both before spinning myself out of their embrace and floating towards Hannah – who was currently mid face-battle with Link across the diner. I peeled her away from him, stealing her for a dance.

"Ahem!" I cleared my throat in an obnoxiously playful manner as I wiggled up to Hannah and Link.

Hannah peeled herself away from him with a groan. "Can I help you, Ma'am?" She asked with a dramatic eyeroll. Link laughed, releasing her from his hold. He twirled her around and placed a final, delicate kiss on her plump, cherry lips.

"You were off gettin' yours honey, figured I'd get me a little something too." She shimmied her shoulders into me, letting me steal her away from her man for a dance.

"Look at those two," she chuckled, pointing to my boys. I glanced in their direction, soaking in the sight of them dancing together. Teddy wasn't much shorter than Jonas, but the difference in their frames was evident when they were so close.

Jonas soared over 6 feet tall, where Teddy just cut in. Both of my boys were in their Wranglers and Ariats, but just their outfits alone showed their differences.

Teddy's R.M. Williams t-shirt clung to his chest. The fabric stretched across his chest, before falling down his hard stomach and tucking into his belt – exposing his PBR Championship belt. The faded blue Wranglers sat low on his hips, accentuating his muscular ass as they cascaded down his legs, meeting the intricate patterns that adorned his dusty, well-worn boots. Everything about him was just dishevelled enough that he always had a 'bad boy' demeanour. His hair fell messily across his face, now free from the restraints of his hat – which had found a new home on my head.

Several silver rings framed his calloused hands, each an ode to his bull-riding days – except one. The simple band that rested on his left middle finger was a new addition. He had it made several weeks ago, along with the tiny tattoo that now rested next to it on his fourth digit: "R.J."

My eyes trailed to Jonas, who had his hands curled in Teddy's. I scaled his thick, muscular arms, and followed the lines of the dark, flannel shirt that covered his torso. The collar slightly up-turned, resting neatly beneath his well-groomed beard. His hair kept short beneath his hat, which was dipped low on his head, casting shadows across his brows. His jeans – like Teddy's – were well-worn and fit just right; the denim clung to his thighs for dear life. Where Teddy's boots were dusty, Jonas's were polished.

Teddy's deep, growly laugh snapped me out of my trance. My head jerked up and I took in the sight of my men. Jonas twirled Teddy around the dance floor in a bridal waltz, while the two of them laughed hysterically as they argued over who would be the lead. Teddy seemed to have lost that battle considering he was currently being dipped into a kiss by Jonas. I couldn't help but smile at them.

"Red, get your ass over here and show this idiot how it's done!"

I spun away from Hannah, leaving her to return to Link – who was currently dancing with someone's Nana. Gliding across the dance floor, I slid into the warm embrace of my men. The music ripped through my bones and took hold of my feet as I let myself fall into rhythm.

Twenty-Two

Jonas

"Babe, do you know where my fuckin' lighter is?" Teddy called from the balcony. I sighed, shaking my head as I walked to meet him outside, lighter in hand.

"Dude, you need to remember where you put your shit," I chuckled, and handed him the lighter.

"Then what do I have you for, sweet boy?" he purred, wiggling his eyebrows as he sparked his cigarette.

River stumbled through our bedroom door, a huge package in her hands that made her seem even smaller. Our girl was not gifted in the height department. She was our perfect little package.

"Peach. What the actual fuck is that?" Teddy asked, taking a deep drag of his cigarette.

"I will have you know, Theodore, this is a very important artifact," she said, beaming as she tore into the package. Her eyes lit up like a fucking Christmas tree as she pulled a giant, dragon-esque strap-on from the box.

I'm not joking when I tell you that since we officially became... whatever it is we were, she had been *hoarding* toys. It's been a year. You can do the math on how many fucking toys we had.

"Uh... whatcha got there, Red?"

Her honey-like eyes glowed beneath her thick, brown lashes, and her smile only accentuated her delicious dimples. "I wanted to try something different. My current one is boring, and it's my birthday!" she explained, inspecting the toy thoroughly before meeting our gaze with a feral look that took over her face.

"Current one? You have an entire drawer full of shit, Red. And your birthday isn't for a week!" I exclaimed, laughing and shaking my head. These two would be the death of me.

Teddy smiled devilishly, his cigarette held between his lips. I don't know why that was always so sexy, but my cock throbbed painfully against my shorts at the sight.

His voice came out deep and gravelled as he said, "Come on, let her have her fun, Jonas. We both know you prefer to take me anyway."

"Alright boys, who's first?"

TWENTY-THREE
Teddy

My hands instinctively found their own way across Jonas's gorgeous chest as I trailed kisses down his throat. I knew this man's body.

"God, baby, you're so perfect," I moaned against his ear.

River and I worked in tandem, sucking and caressing every inch of him, lavishing him with our touch as he laid there on our bed. The soft, growly moans seeping from his lips sent a rush of blood straight to my already hard cock.

He reached for me, hungrily wrapping his hand around my girth. He began working my dick in time with River, who was tear-soaked and stuffed full of him. Her mouth looked so pretty with his cock in it.

"Good girl. Cry for us, Peach," I groaned, before my mouth met Jonas's. His tongue massaged my own firmly as he pumped my cock, thrusting himself into River's throat. Watching them together made me fucking crazy.

River popped him out of her mouth, her swollen lips creeping into a wicked smile as she reached for the new strap-on she'd purchased. She slid herself into the harness, securing the toy in place as she squirted a liberal amount of lube across its ridges. She trailed kisses up Jonas's chest, meeting me on the other side of his neck, and slid her hands across his hips.

"I want you to suck Teddy's cock while I fuck you," she demanded, never breaking eye contact with me.

"Bossy girl, Peach." I smirked wickedly as I replaced Jonas's hand with my own and stroked myself. His eyes lit up as he watched me pump my cock in his face. Such a good boy.

"Come here, baby," he moaned, bringing his mouth to my tip. I pushed my cock past his rough lips, plunging deep into his throat. Shivers crept over my spine, and I felt the sweet sense of Nirvana wash over me as I bottomed out inside him.

"Good, fucking, boy!" I panted, thrusting myself deeper into him. River watched us, stroking more lube across the toy. She always liked to watch. Filthy girl.

"Come on, Peach. Show me how you fuck him."

She positioned herself between his thick, muscular thighs and leant forward to kiss me. She lined herself up to his tight, rear entrance, steadying herself as she pushed the tip of the toy into his ass. His deep moans sent vibrations up my cock; my balls twitched at the sensation.

"God, you're perfect," I told him, stroking his face as I fucked his dirty mouth. I slapped my palm down across his bearded cheek and he whimpered in approval. Good boy.

River adjusted herself as he stretched to accommodate the large, ribbed toy. She slowly worked herself deeper, until she bottomed out inside him. Her smile was devious as she held his waist and settled herself into him. She rested for a moment, allowing him to stretch to her size before she began bucking her hips, filling him beautifully.

Our bodies entwined and we became one. Jonas was stuffed fully with both of our cocks, and tears fell from his eyes as he took me in his mouth. He hadn't bottomed very often – this whole dynamic was still new for all of us. Jonas had only been with one man, me. And fuck did I love teaching him how to take my cock, and River's.

Our little Peach was becoming quite the power top. I loved watching her explore her own confidence. When she strapped up, she got a wicked sparkle in her eye. It was like her inner beast was unleashed. The way she used us for her own pleasure. It drove Jonas and I fucking wild.

"You keep fucking him like that, Peach, and I'm gonna come," I growled.

Her eyes flashed a darker shade of honey as she reached between her legs. The toy sprung to life, intense vibrations shooting through all of us.

Jonas ripped himself from my cock. "Oh, fuck, Red!"

I don't know if it was the sight of them together, or the intense face-fucking I was giving him, but the second his eyes rolled back in his skull, I spilled my load in ribbons across him. River smiled, picking up the pace as she ground herself into Jonas.

"Good boy. Take me. Stretch for me, baby." Her breathy pants were enough to send shockwaves through my spent cock.

I took her face in my hands and snarled, "Peach, if you keep spitting filthy words from that pretty mouth of yours, I'm going to stuff my cock so far down your throat you'll need a fucking oxygen tank." Her body reacted deliciously. Tears pooled in her eyes as I gripped her jaw in my hands and squeezed.

I leant in to kiss her as she pumped one final thrust into our man, and Jonas spilled his own release over his stomach. River slowly eased out of him, and we collapsed together on our bed. She got to work on cleaning our spend from Jonas, giggling and kissing him as she went.

I sparked another cigarette and smiled as they curled up and started talking about whatever insane adventure they wanted to go on someday. Inhaling deeply, I let the cool air nip at my face, and as I sucked down the tendrils of smoke, I watched them together. Smiling. Laughing. Planning the future... our future.

My man.

My woman.

My world.

With a deep sigh, I looked down over them. "I love you."

They both smiled up at me. "We know."

TWENTY-FOUR
Teddy

"Get your ass over here, Peach. The cattle ain't gonna muster themselves, baby," I shout at River from the saddle of my mount.

Harley had been my ride since I was a teenager; we basically grew up together. He was 17 now, and getting on in his years, but he could run with the best of them. As a burly, chestnut stock horse, his coat was the same, deep red as River's hair. It gave me a sense of comfort.

Jonas's deep chuckle rang through my ears as he trotted up behind me on his own horse. Being a retired racehorse, Avalon was the tallest of our three horses. He was also the only buckskin in Fires Creek. He was a wild, free-spirited, young stallion, and boy did he remind Jonas of his youth every chance he got. Funnily enough, our horses were complete opposites, kind of like us in a way.

"Nice boots, Red." Jonas smirked and wiggled his eyebrows at River as he took his place next to me.

"Fuck off, you two," she replied, as she stumbled out of the stables as she pulled her boots over her now well-worn jeans. The Almighty Alex had taken one of the lead ropes off the work bench and somehow wrapped it, and himself around one of River's legs. The sight of her falling ass-over-tit on top of our dog was bloody hilarious. She looked less than impressed as she untangled herself from him and scratched the sweet spot behind his ear. River surprised everyone, mostly herself, I think. She'd dived straight into the farm after her first night here, learning the ropes and contributing to the workload. It was like she was the missing piece of our puzzle.

Jonas helped her brush up on her riding skills, *in more ways than one, if you catch my drift*. She had become a brilliant little rider; she and Scout were made for each other. Scout was the 15-year-old bay mare that we picked up a few months before River arrived – along with our surprise, bonus foal, Lenny – but she had met her match with River. They were two peas in one chaotic pod.

River wandered over to Scout, taking the reins, and lifting her foot into the stirrup before mounting in one fluid motion. She straightened her shirt and sat herself comfortably in the saddle. Nudging her heels into Scout's withers, she pulled out onto the stock route with a content look on her face.

"Come on boys, let's ride!' she shouted, tipping her hat.

We motioned our own horses on and met River's pace as we moved into a canter, making our way towards the cattle yards. We had a 3-day muster ahead of us, our saddle bags were bursting at the seams. Alex followed closely behind us. Despite his age, he still came on musters with us. I dreaded the day when he stayed home, knowing it would likely be because he had decided his time was coming to an end. He trotted wearily behind the horses, the spring in his step fading day by day.

The first few days after River's arrival was spent lazily fucking, cooking, and dancing as we rode out the storm together and found our footing as a throuple. None of us really discussed things, but it felt so right for us to all be together. River melted us, and we succumbed to her every whim. She allowed Jonas and me time to explore this new side of our relationship, and be – what it turns out – we'd both always wanted to be. I'd been with men before, but it'd never been like this. I'd never felt this way about *anyone* before. Not until River arrived in Fires Creek and gave me the courage to take my shot. River and Jonas were my soulmates, we loved each other, and that's all I needed to know.

I watched my woman as she rode on ahead of me, edging the cattle and smiling back at us, meeting my gaze. "Stop staring at my ass, Theodore James!" she shouted behind a laugh as she rode off into the sunrise.

I smiled freely and watched as her hair flowed in the gentle breeze, and she had never looked so beautiful.

TWENTY-FIVE

Jonas

We'd been riding for hours as we rounded the cattle into the stockyard, setting up camp just off the stock route. This was a usual site for us on this muster – with accessible stockyards, a creek nearby, and plenty of trees to shade the horses and cattle.

River tied Scout to a post, dismounted, and began untacking her. She whistled a tune as she slid the saddle across the mare's rump, resting the well-worn leather against the tree. She pulled a cloth from her saddle bag, and gently washed under Scout's belly, where her girth sat.

Teddy and I moved to work on unsaddling and tying up our own horses, stealing kisses, and playfully whipping each other with the reins. He never failed to bring a smile to my face. It was like we were kindred spirits roaming freely on this Earth. Being with him made me feel so *seen*, so alive.

River and her effervescence balanced out my grouchy ways, and seemed to subdue the inner devil that consumed Teddy's every waking breath. His playboy demeanour disappeared the moment she stepped foot in Fires Creek. She was the light in the darkness. She was *ours*, and we were *hers*.

I watched quietly as she removed her jeans and hung them over her saddle to air, then slid her cropped t-shirt over her full, perky tits. She peeled her bra and panties from her delicious curves, her tits springing to life as they released from her bra. Discarding her garments, she stood there – naked and exposed to us in all her glory – before winking at us and announced cheekily, "Swim time, boys!"

She strolled casually down the hill to the large creek at the foot of the mountain below, still whistling her tune as she slipped herself into the crystal water. "Well, are you coming?" she shouted up at us, then dipped herself under the water, and flipped her hair back, like some kind of mermaid. *God, she'd be a sexy mermaid.*

"Don't have to tell me twice," Teddy called in response. I don't know how I missed that mother fucker stripping, but he bolted – stark naked – cackling like a madman as he ran towards River. A wicked smile was plastered on his gorgeous face, as his bare ass glowed in the afternoon sun.

I couldn't help but grin happily as I watched him dive into the creek. The wave his body created showered River as he splashed into the pristine pool of water before us. I removed my clothes as I watched them play in the creek. River's laugh echoed through the silent paddock like gentle wind chimes, and the sound went straight to my dick.

"Move over, bitches!" I yowled, running towards them, now naked myself. I half tripped over a low-lying branch, and face planted into the creek. The pair of them nearly drowned from laughing at me. I came up for air, and ran my calloused palm through my beard as I lunged for River. With my arms outstretched, I pulled her into my chest, and, like always, her body fit perfectly against mine.

She raised her face to me, the pools of gold beneath her lashes swirled with a devilish twinkle as she pressed her lips to mine. Our mouths became one as she slipped her tongue between my lips, and the kiss became hungrier. She pulled herself up, wrapping her legs around me, and I held her there. She ran her fingers through my wet hair as she deepened our kiss and bucked her pussy into me.

"Well, well, well, you two," Teddy snickered, wading closer to us with his usual wicked smile. Dark lust enveloped his soft, brown eyes as he slid behind River. I felt his hands wash over her ass as he slipped his fingers inside her throbbing cunt. Her moans vibrated over my tongue, and she let herself fall into pleasure.

"Good girl, Peach."

I guided my hard cock gently into her warm centre, replacing Teddy's fingers. A sharp exhale escaped her mouth as she stretched to accommodate my size. Teddy smiled behind her, moving her hair to one shoulder and biting down into the curve of her tattooed neck.

"Now, Little Peach, Relax," he purred, lifting her slightly higher on my dick. She arched her back ever so slightly to give me better access to her perfect tits. Teddy's hand wrapped around her, resting on her waist. I felt him stabilise himself as he eased his cock into her tight ass. He groaned loudly, with his eyes rolling back into his head as he worked himself deeper into her.

"Good fucking girl. You're so full, Peach. Take us all, let us *own* you," he panted. His rhythm increased as she adjusted to us both filling her tight, greedy holes. His praise and dominance drove me fucking wild. I could feel his cock pressing against mine as we were inside her together, stretching her so beautifully.

"Oh, god, fuck yes!" She screamed, bucking wildly as we held her between us, pounding into her. The cool waters of the creek gave her throbbing cunt a brief release from the brutal fucking. I grabbed her breast in my hand, squeezing hard and rolling her pierced nipple through my fingers as she quivered against my touch. Her cunt clamped against my cock, stretched to its limit from my girth.

"Red, *fuck*, baby. You look so perfect stuffed with us. I love you," I whimpered into her. My thrusts became feral and desperate. Teddy's balls slapped against mine while we fucked her in tandem.

"I love you too," she breathed, then her body gave out as she twitched between us. She arched back into Teddy, baring her tits to me as she panted, "I love you, Teddy. I love you both."

Teddy picked up his pace, plunging himself into her. We held her still, using each other as support as we fucked her. We both found our release together and spilled ourselves into our girl. She convulsed against us, her own orgasm taking her until she became weak in our arms. Completely spent, she nestled her head against my chest, while soft whimpers escaped her swollen lips.

We slipped out of her, the embrace extending as we both kissed her forehead softly. Teddy leaned into me, planting a playful kiss on my cheek before he whispered, "I love you, too, you know?"

"I know," I replied.

We cuddled there in the still waters for what felt like an eternity as the sun left the sky and was replaced by the moon.

"The sunset looks so beautiful reflecting off the water," River said.

"That's why they named the town Fires Creek, Peach."

"Really?" she asked.

"Yep. They say the founders of the town saw the reflection of the sunset on the water and thought their crops were on fire. Once they realised what happened, they named the town after it," I explained.

"Fires Creek," she stated contemplatively.

"The very same," Teddy replied.

We emerged from the creek, the night air fresh against our naked bodies. We helped each other dress before we set up for dinner and curled up by the fire. Alex wandered over, taking a seat on the rug next to River and resting his weary head against her knee.

"I love you, Teddy," I murmured.

"I know," came his reply.

We let the silence linger as the stars danced in the country sky, the only sound was the rustling leaves of the trees and the cattle lowing nearby.

Knowing where I am, where I'm going, and who I was wrapped up with, I felt safe. I felt happy. I felt *home*.

EPILOGUE
River

1 year later

I stormed out of the house, straight down to the shed, and shouted over the noise of the engine roaring. "Theodore James and Jonas Carter, move your asses or we're going to be late!" The beat-up Ford they were under had definitely seen better days.

Bang!

"Ah! Fuck me!" came the oh-so-familiar, husky voice that spilled from Jonas's lips.

Teddy slid out from underneath the vehicle on his spinney... roller... mechanic man thing – you know the one I mean. A wicked smile danced over his face and enveloped his eyes as he winked at me and chuckled.

"What have you done, Theodore?" I asked, pretending to be huffy.

Jonas slid out on his own fancy thingamajig, rubbing his head as he flashed me an equally evil smile. They wiggled their eyebrows and both shouted in unison, "Surprise!" *Fucking hell.*

"I told you both already: birthdays absolutely suck, and I do not want a party!" I grumbled.

"Oh, come on, Red! Don't be like that, your cheeks are about to match your hair," Jonas bellowed, both he and Teddy hysterically laughing. Idiots. *My idiots.*

"Yeah, Peach," Teddy grinned, slapping my ass as he strutted cockily out of the shed and made his way towards the house.

"Yoohoo, River, my dear!" came the shrill voice of none other than our closest neighbour, Brenda.

"You invited fucking *Brenda*," I hissed at Jonas quietly, punching him in the arm before extending my own to our neighbour.

"Hi, Mrs Huntford."

"I am here to collect you for your surprise party!" she cooed glee-fully, taking my hand and whisking me away to the house. I wagged my other arm angrily towards Jonas as I let the old woman drag me inside. *Surprise my ass. The boys hadn't stopped talking about it for days.*

A few hours later, I was hauled over to The Jensen's place down the road, along with the whole of Fires Creek and their dogs. *Literally. This is the country folks.* My men cheerfully greeted everyone, working in tandem to command the crowd.

Jonas had really come out of his shell. Since being with us, he just seemed so... content. I watched him twirl someone's Nana around the dance floor before Teddy cut in and they guided each other across the room. I loved watching them; they were so different together. Teddy's usual devilish behaviour was much more subdued these days, but he never held back on Jonas. He was always riding his ass, sometimes literally.

Over the past few months, we'd been exploring our relationships and ourselves. We never really *came out;* we just continued with our lives. Only now, we did it together. We all made time to be alone, and to be together as individual couples. But every night, we always ended up with the three of us together. I couldn't really explain how, when, or why we worked, we just *did*. Where one of us lacked, the other exceeded. We were a team, a unit. We were *us*.

"Daydreaming again, Peach?" Teddy breathed into my neck as he slid around me and pulled me onto the dancefloor. Jonas's arm stretched out to meet ours. We twirled and laughed like absolute fools. The sun set over the rolling mountains behind us as we danced and drank with our neighbours and friends.

In the 18-months since I had been in Fires Creek, it had become more like home than anywhere else I had ever been. The town banded together like a single entity, always looking out for each other. Nobody even seemed surprised by Jonas and Teddy, considering it was such a small country town.

The boys never hid their feelings towards each other, often walking hand in hand through the town square. They were so unapologetically in love, it made me thankful to be part of them. So, while people always asked about me, they never looked differently at the men they'd known their whole lives.

We had all been through our fair share of hard times. I think we all needed to work through some shit, but we had all the time in the world for that. The past year had been a whirlwind of new experiences and opportunities I never thought I would have.

In such a short time, I had gone from a miserable, overpaid designer, living in a fancy apartment with a cheating leach. To the owner of a working farm, living in a manor, with two wonderful men who treated me like royalty. And I own a fucking horse! I still couldn't believe life had turned out the way it did, but I couldn't be happier.

"I love you," I said.

"We know," they said back as they swept me through the barn doors, and we made the slow walk back home.

The End

ACKNOWLEDGEMENTS

First and foremost, I want to thank my wonderful husband, Ben, for the late-night cups of tea, glasses of wine, and snacks. Your never-ending support of me and my publishing journey, while we navigate parenthood and full-time jobs. How you never doubted me, even when I doubted myself. I could not have finished this book without you. You are the most wonderful and caring partner, father, and friend and I love you.

I started this journey on maternity leave, with no real plans of ever publishing – or any idea of what to expect from this journey, but I have loved every minute. Every giggle. Every tear. Every hour spent curled up, typing furiously and yelling into the void.

I want to thank my ALPHA readers, Clarisce and Ashley. Your love, support, and never-ending unhinged comments kept me going. I am so grateful that I found you both, this book would never have made it into people's hands without your guidance.

To my BETA readers, ARC team, and Street Team. Thank you from the bottom of my heart for loving and hyping my spicy little novella. I am so grateful to have you in my corner.

To my PA, Misha Taylor, for trying to wrangle my chaos.

To my editor, Erin Page, I could literally not have done this without you.

To the friends I have made along my bookstagram journey, and venturing into the world of self-publishing, thank you.

To my readers, thank you for giving Fires Creek a chance. I appreciate you.

Thank you, Peach.

ABOUT THE AUTHOR
D.M. Henderson

D.M. Henderson is a happily married mum of 2 from rural Australia. She has 2 cavoodles and a toothless cat. She loves cheese, wine, coffee, board games, and chaotic dance parties.

You will often find her with her nose in a book (or her kindle) and a cosy blanket. Her first dive into the world of erotic romance were the 'Divas' novels by Rebecca Chance.

After joining the 'Bookstagram' community as an influencer during her maternity leave, she was quickly enamored with indie authors, and the romance genre which prompted her to write her debut, *Fires Creek*.

She writes wild hearts, and whiskey-fuelled cowboys with filthy mouths who take what's theirs and are guaranteed to make you swoon.

ALSO BY
D.M. Henderson

TROPES:
SMALL TOWN ROMANCE
COWBOY/WESTERN
STRANGERS TO LOVERS
WIDOWER/SINGLE DAD MMC
ALT/MUSIC TEACHER FMC
FOUND FAMILY
RURAL AUSTRALIAN SETTING
AGE GAP
DUAL POV
BOOK 1 OF A DUET

READ NOW

TROPES:
SMALL TOWN ROMANCE
COWBOY/WESTERN
FOUND FAMILY
DUAL POV
BOOK 2 OF A DUET

PREORDER NOW

www.ingramcontent.com/pod-product-compliance
Lightning Source LLC
Chambersburg PA
CBHW061456210726

48287CB00007B/2527